The victim appeared to be a teenage boy. His crumpled body, lying almost dead center in the alley, looked oddly flat and somehow lonely despite the number of people surrounding it. The flashing red light on the ambulance parked near him washed across his face at regular intervals, turning his blood-smeared features an ugly magenta color. His hair, shorter than usual for someone his age, was matted with some greasy substance that was also smeared all over the front of his T-shirt. Both his feet were bare, blood spattered and filthy dirty.

He didn't look real either, which was good, as dead bodies are not my thing.

★

Forthcoming from Worldwide Mystery by
E. L. LARKIN

HEAR ME DIE
DIE AND DIE
DEAD MEN DIE

HEAR MY CRY
E. L. LARKIN

WORLDWIDE.®

TORONTO • NEW YORK • LONDON
AMSTERDAM • PARIS • SYDNEY • HAMBURG
STOCKHOLM • ATHENS • TOKYO • MILAN
MADRID • WARSAW • BUDAPEST • AUCKLAND

HEAR MY CRY

A Worldwide Mystery/July 2001

First published by Thomas Bouregy & Company, Inc.

ISBN 0-373-26391-0

Printed in U.S.A.

HEAR MY CRY

ONE

HE DIDN'T LOOK LIKE a potential victim.

He looked like a middle-aged male chauvinist. A large man, not fat, just large, with hard brown eyes and the positive manner of a man accustomed to having his own way. His name was Peter Johnson. I met him in a perfectly ordinary way. He called on a Monday morning right after the Fourth of July and asked for an appointment at one-thirty the following day. He arrived a little ahead of time.

Dressed in a navy pinstripe suit, cream-colored silk shirt, and Armani tie, he also looked like a man with money.

Martha showed him into my office, where he stopped just inside the door by the citrus-colored wool wall hanging and gave me a surprised look. "Are you Demary Jones?" he asked in a sharp voice.

I always try to be courteous, at least to start with, so I had already stood up and started around the end of my desk. His attitude stopped me right there. "Yes, I'm Demary Jones," I said. "What were you expecting?"

"I thought you were a man."

"Named Demary?" Actually, it *is* a man's name, but I wasn't about to admit that to him. It was my Scottish grandfather's name. He pronounced it Dem-ry. I pronounce it De-mary.

"The way it's spelled, it could be a man's name," Peter Johnson said, frowning at me.

"Yes, it could, but in this case it isn't. And you can go out the same way you came in if my sex bothers you. The door is right behind you." I smiled at him, keeping my tone light, but I meant what I said. I have a redhead's temper, and the implied put-down lit my fuse.

For a moment I thought he would leave, then he laughed, a harsh bark of sound that reminded me of a seal. He walked across the room and got one of the tangerine-colored leather chairs from against the wall. "Sit down," he said, seating himself.

I thought again about telling him to leave, but for all his bad manners he was wearing an Armani outfit that had set him back a hunk of change. I have an unfortunate weakness for money.

Mentally boosting my fee, I went back around my desk and sat down facing him.

"I see I've angered you," he said. "Well, that doesn't matter. We don't have to like each other in order to work together."

His stock went up a notch. That happened to be one of my pet beliefs.

"I want you to tap a telephone," he said. "*My* telephone."

For a moment I was too surprised to answer. "That's illegal," I said finally.

"I said it was my telephone."

"It's still illegal." I didn't know whether it was or not at the time and I doubted if he knew either. "What telephone, anyway? Your home or business?"

"My office phone."

"Have your secretary listen in."

"I don't want Miss Wagoner to know about it."

I shrugged. I was curious, I always am, but tapping telephones wasn't in my bag of tricks. My mechanical and/or electrical knowledge is zip, and I don't know anyone in that line either.

"This *is* Confidential Research and Inquiry, isn't it? You are a private investigator, aren't you?" he demanded.

"No, not really, and certainly not the kind you seem to want. I do research, just like it says on the door. Individual research such as genealogy, historical research for writers, and some legal research for attorneys."

"What kind of writers? What kind of research do you do for them?"

I shrugged. "Mostly romance writers. But at the moment I'm doing some work for a biographer, researching clothing terms used in England during the eleventh century. I don't tap telephones. I wouldn't even if I knew how. Why do you want it done?"

"That's none of your business."

"You're right," I said, giving him a smirk that showed my teeth. I hadn't liked him to start with and he was making it easy to ignore his better qualities. "I'm afraid you have the wrong agency, Mr. Johnson." I stood up and circled around to the door.

He didn't move. "You come highly recommended by a man I trust," he said calmly. "You have a private investigator's license and I don't have time to find anyone else. I want it done right now. I, uh, I think my secretary is having an affair with my son and I want to know for sure."

He was a poor liar. "So? What's your objection?" I asked, wondering who in the world had ever recommended me to him. "Is the woman your property?"

"No, I'm a married man," he said, his voice curiously prudish. "But I'm also a businessman.

My son may be into something that will ruin my company, but I need to be sure before I do…before I go any further.''

That sounded like it might be the truth. ''Then you don't necessarily need your phone tapped,'' I told him. ''What you need is a—''

He interrupted me with an angry gesture. ''I want my phone tapped, and I want a recording made.''

I opened the door. ''Good-bye, Mr. Johnson.''

Martha was moving boxes around in the storage closet next door; one of them fell over with a crash, so I didn't hear what he said next but I didn't care. I simply shook my head and opened the door a little wider.

Face flushing with anger, he got up and marched across the room. He stopped in front of me for a moment as if he meant to say something else, then went on across the reception room and jerked open the outside door. The two, my office door and the one to the street, are in a direct line.

The first shot hit the casing beside my head with an ugly *twang*. Splinters spewed in all directions.

The next two shots hit Mr. Johnson in the chest. He lurched sideways, clawing at the door frame, turned, and staggered several steps back into the room.

"Luck is a ventry fly!" he cried. Or at least that's what it sounded like to me. The next shot hit him in the back and he fell forward onto the rug, his expression surprised and slightly peevish.

Then something hit my head. It didn't hurt; it was more like a thunderclap. A huge dark wave of sound rushed toward me and I felt myself sliding into a gulf of nothingness. In those last seconds I heard someone screaming and knew, with a kind of distant interest, that it was Martha. She wasn't the screaming type and I wondered what she was yelling about.

WHEN I OPENED my eyes someone had painted my ceiling a pale pastel green. I hate pastel colors. I'd like to say my whole life passed before my eyes as I lay there, or that I experienced some kind of a new awakening, but nothing of the sort occurred. I was angry about the paint job, but before I could get too upset the color changed to pale mauve, began to turn in gentle circles, and that was that.

The next time I opened my eyes the green ceiling was still there but I wasn't interested. My head hurt so bad nothing else mattered.

A starchy voice said, "She's coming out of it."

Someone picked up my wrist. Their fingers were cold and dry.

"Demary." A man called my name in a hard, penetrating voice.

The room shifted, tilted, and for a moment came into soft focus. Lieutenant Sam Morgan from the Seattle PD homicide division was standing beside my bed. He and I are old friends, of a sort. We go back to when I was a kid living on the street, to when I still believed in flower power. He said something, asked me something, but the words were just sounds without any meaning.

I was suddenly and violently sick to my stomach. Before I could do more than turn my head I threw up. When I got my breath back I slid into a free-floating world where I could hear and feel the people around me but I didn't have any urge to know who they were, what they were doing, or what they wanted.

Someone wiped my face and neck with a cold wet cloth. It felt so good I nearly cried, something I don't very often do. I realized I was in a hospital and then, abruptly, I remembered what had happened and knew I'd been shot.

"Miss Jones, can you hear me?" the starched presence asked.

I made my mouth form the word yes. I didn't open my eyes. My head felt like it was going to explode.

"All right. You may talk to her for three minutes," another voice said. "No more."

"Demary, listen to me. You've got to help me. You've got to answer me," Sam said, speaking slowly and clearly. "Do you understand me, Demary?"

It took a lot of effort but I finally got my eyes open and told him yes, I understood.

"Demary, did you see who fired the shots?" Sam took my hand in his and stroked it gently.

"No. Only...only Johnson." It was hard to get the words out.

"Do you know where Martha went?"

The room started slipping away again.

"Demary! Demary, don't pass out on me. I've got to know about Martha," he said, sounding anxious now. "What happened to her?"

"She screamed."

"Demary, Peter Johnson is dead and Martha Kingman has disappeared. She may have been kidnapped. Can you tell me anything, remember anything, anything at all, that will help find her?"

I tried to tell him no but I drifted off without saying it. I heard the stiff voice say something in an angry murmur but the words were just a noise in the distance.

THE THIRD TIME I woke I felt better. My head still hurt but it wasn't anywhere near as bad as it had been before. The room was dim and quiet. A young woman in a nurse's uniform stood changing an IV bottle beside my bed that was connected to a needle taped to my wrist.

"Hello. Are you back among us?" she asked.

"I think so." I turned my head cautiously, trying to see the rest of the room. "What time is it?"

"Eight o'clock in the evening. And I'd be careful about moving my head too much if I were you. It's liable to start pounding pretty sharpish. You were hit by a rifle bullet. The slug barely grazed you, they only took three stitches, but it gave you quite a wallop. You're going to hurt for a while."

"Why am I so sick?" I meant weak but the word didn't come to me.

"Shock and loss of blood. Head wounds bleed something fierce."

She finished with the IV bottle and picked up my wrist to take my pulse. In a minute she gave me a conspiratorial smile. "Don't tell anyone I told you so, but by tomorrow afternoon you should feel pretty much all right except for a thundering headache."

I smiled back. My face felt stiff. "I thought

nurses were the stern, silent type. Never told anybody anything.''

''I think that's the Navy submarine service,'' she said, winking at me. ''Anyway, I always figure the patient has as much right to know what's going on as I have.''

She took my blood pressure, noted it on a chart, and gathered up her things. ''Oh, by the way, there's a police officer waiting outside to talk to you. Do you want to see her or shall I just walk on by?''

''No, send her in, please. I want to know what happened to my secretary.''

The officer was a young black woman. She opened the door quietly and tiptoed across to my bed. Her looks startled me for a moment. She looked like Martha, except that she was a good twenty years younger and not quite as tall. Martha is an even six foot, with Grecian features, close-cropped black hair, and a broad English accent.

''Hello, I'm Sergeant Clausen,'' this one said as she came up to me. ''Lieutenant Morgan has some questions... Good grief!'' She stared at me with a startled expression. ''They shaved off half your hair.''

She looked so shocked I pushed myself up a little and tried to see in the vanity across the room.

"Here." She dug around in her shoulder bag and handed me a mirror.

To polish up an old cliché, I really couldn't believe my eyes. They actually had shaved off half my hair. I looked ridiculous. One side of my head was its usual mass of short curls. The other side was painted orange and was as bare as an egg except for a two-inch-square bandage.

"What an absolutely rotten thing to do," Sergeant Clausen said. "They didn't need to do that."

I agreed and then some. The doctor could have made do with a much smaller working space. I've certainly never been a raving beauty, but with that hairdo I looked grotesque.

I'm five foot two and at least ten pounds overweight, with naturally curly reddish-brown hair and a rosy complexion. All of which tends to make me look like a middle-aged Little Orphan Annie, a big asset sometimes. No one takes an investigator seriously when she reminds them of a comic strip. My looks make ferreting out information ridiculously easy sometimes.

But a female Kojak? I'd be a laughingstock.

TWO

SERGEANT CLAUSEN—her given name was Jean—had a whole notebook full of questions Sam Morgan wanted settled. Unfortunately, I didn't have any answers for him.

There wasn't much she could tell me either. According to her, Sam and his men had not only not found Martha, they didn't have a clue as to where she'd gone, or been taken. Impossible as it seemed, no one had seen her leave the office—walking, carried, dragged, or whatever. Several people, including myself, had heard her scream, but no one had actually seen what happened to her. By the time the first person in authority reached me, Martha was nowhere around.

"Several people heard the shots, but mostly they didn't recognize them as gunshots, or know where they came from." Jean shrugged. "So far, we don't know where they came from either. The first person to realize something was wrong was a woman passerby who glanced in the open doorway. She saw Johnson lying on the floor in a pool of blood and ran to the drugstore. The druggist called 911 and from then on it was routine.''

"How crazy. Someone should have seen the guy, or the car if it was a drive-by.''

"Yes, and particularly the woman who first saw Johnson. She thinks she may have heard the shots as she came out of the bakery down the street and she should have seen something of the shooter, but she says she didn't see anything unusual at all. No one running, no one carrying anything that could have been a gun, no suspicious car, nothing. And it couldn't have been more than a minute or two between the time the shots were fired and when she saw Johnson.''

Jean hesitated, looking down at her feet. "I should have recognized the sound of the shots myself. I think I did hear them, but I didn't realize what they were.''

"You heard the shots? Where were you?''

"In my accountant's office. Harry Madison. He's in the same building you are. I had parked down on Forty-third, though, so I came in and left through his back door.''

Actually, five businesses share the building with me. We share the front reception room too, where Martha works. We even share Martha to some extent. I'm her primary employer but she does a lot of computer work for the other tenants. Which is fine with me, as I couldn't afford to pay her what she's worth on my own. All the offices have an individual private entrance also at the back of the building alongside our parking lot. Mine is at the corner facing the side street.

"How, or when, did you learn what had happened?" I asked.

"When I went to work at six o'clock."

"It happens that way sometimes," I said, giving a small shrug that nearly tore my head off. For a minute I couldn't even breathe. When I could hear again she was saying:

"I should have recognized the sound immediately but I've been so nervous and jumpy lately I guess I just didn't...." She made a wry face.

"What have you been nervous about?" She didn't look like the skittish type.

She gave an embarrassed little laugh. "Someone has been following me. For several weeks. And even though I know I'm being silly, it bothers me. Especially as I can't get a make on them."

I grinned. "Maybe a would-be swain?"

"Swain? *Swain?* Good grief. I haven't heard that word since my grandmother died. But no, I don't think so. Probably just my imagination."

"Occupational hazard."

Jean nodded.

She was getting ready to leave when I had another visitor. Sam Morgan's son, Howie, knocked and stuck his head around the edge of the door. Howie graduated several years ago from the University of Texas at El Paso, but he had only recently joined the police force here in Seattle. He was still a rookie patrolman.

He came inside with a cheerful greeting for me and a rakish wink for the sergeant.

Jean gave him a somewhat tentative smile. She seemed startled and ill at ease, making me wonder if she knew him on a personal level. I've known Howie in a distant way for a long time simply because I know his father, but we aren't friends. I don't particularly like him. He's one of those people who always give me the impression they're running some kind of a scam, although Howie has never been in any kind of trouble that I know of.

"Don't mind me," he told the sergeant. "I just came by to see how Demary was doing." He gave us both his big white-toothed smile, but he had his eye on Jean. Howie is a good-looking guy if you like the ultra-sophisticated type. He has his uniforms tailor-made, works on his tan, and Sam had spent a fortune on his orthodontic work.

I'd never known him to have any interest in me

before. I couldn't imagine him caring about my health, and I was feeling just lousy enough to point that out to him, but before I could say anything he went on.

"You're in my precinct, you know. Of course, I'm not part of the investigating team but when Dad told me you'd been shot I thought I'd check it out. He said you had no idea who did it. Is that right?"

"No, I didn't see anyone." His having a professional interest in the shooting sounded a lot more plausible than his having any interest in how I felt. Despite his father's position he had to start at the bottom. If he could contribute to an ongoing case, however, it would be a big step up for him.

"Was Johnson a regular client?" he asked.

"No, I never saw him before, and to save you your next question, I don't know what he wanted either. He came in at about one-thirty—Martha's log will have the exact time—and he was leaving roughly ten minutes later. We didn't do much more than exchange names. I didn't like his attitude and he didn't like mine so we never got around to his reason for coming."

I don't know why I didn't tell them about Johnson wanting the wiretap. I just didn't. Howie asked a couple of more questions but I didn't have any answers to them either, and when the nurse came in to give me a shot, both he and the sergeant left.

I dozed for the next couple of hours, and then around midnight I came out of it with a clear head. I woke up with the whole Peter Johnson thing sharp and distinct in my mind. I remembered every word said, and even the peculiar expression on his face when the last shot hit him. It couldn't have been more than ten seconds, if that long, before I got hit myself, but in those last few moments I'd swear he was pleading with me for something. The few garbled words he cried out as he fell didn't make any sense, though. As far as I could remember he'd yelled something about luck being a fly, or a lie.

In fact, now that I had the time to think, none of it made much sense. The two things didn't fit. According to everything I'd been told, Martha's disappearance, or kidnapping, had been an expert job, but the shooting had been done with a hunting rifle. A professional would never use a gun that size. The hit was poorly organized and conceived too. Two o'clock on a busy thoroughfare is an awkward time and place to use a rifle.

My office building is an old rattletrap of a place in the Wallingford business district. At that hour of the day Forty-fifth Street, which it faces on, is crowded with people. I didn't see how anyone could even carry a rifle around there without being noticed, let alone fire one five times. Yet that was apparently what had happened.

I've lived and worked in the district almost my entire life. My parents' home was on Forty-second. (At the moment they are having a wonderful time seeing the country in a Winnebago.)

I got mixed up with a flower-power group when I graduated from high school, but it didn't take me long to find out real life isn't anything like the dream peddlers say it is. So I went back to school and eventually earned a degree in historical research. My first job was doing title research for a real estate firm just a block down the street from where I am now.

Then I met, fell in love with, and went to work for George Crane. George owned Confidential Research and Inquiry, or C.R.I., which at that time was a private-eye place. I started out as a general assistant but George insisted I get a PI license. He taught me what I know of the business. He never let me do anything at all dangerous, not even any night surveillance, but to everyone's surprise, including my own, I turned out to be good at some of the work. I'm a natural-born snoop.

Then George was killed in a senseless drive-by

shooting and I inherited C.R.I. by default. George had no known relatives and the only business assets were a filing cabinet, some beat-up old furniture, and two years to go on a favorable lease. So I put my name on the door and I've been there ever since. I did buy all new furniture.

George was the one who actually introduced me to Sam Morgan, although I'd known Sam by sight for a number of years. We have a somewhat curious relationship. We argue and fight a lot but we've always been friends, sometimes a bit more than that, but, so far, never romantically involved.

Lying there in the dark with my head aching I was glad I knew Sam. He was someone I could count on and I was frightened.

Whatever else I may or may not be, I'm no hero, and I don't pretend to be. Martha's disappearance had me scared, both for her and for myself.

Everyone assumed Peter Johnson had been the target and that I had been hit accidentally. I was afraid it was the other way around.

I have a gun, a .32, and a license to carry it, but I very seldom take it out of the locked cupboard where I keep it hidden. George insisted that I get one but I don't knowingly take on the kind of job that means carrying a gun. However, a current investigation had turned out to be something more than I expected. The client had hired me to verify the provenance of a painting he was thinking of purchasing. I'll call him the traditional X—clients are entitled to anonymity, even the worst of them. His was a rather unusual request so, along with checking on the painting, I checked on Mr. X.

As I said before, I'm a natural-born snoop.

X is a wealthy and powerful man, but he isn't what you would call a sterling character. That came out in a fairly routine way and at the time I didn't think X was aware of what I'd learned, but now I was beginning to wonder. I didn't see how anyone connected with Johnson would have reason to kidnap Martha—*if* she had been kidnapped—but X had a darn good reason for getting rid of both of us. Martha had actually been the one who unearthed much of the dirt in his background.

I'm good with computers, very good, but I sometimes think Martha has microchips for brains. She's a genius at locating any kind of documented information and most of my work is just that, digging out records of one kind or another. Even finding a missing person, something I do occasionally, is usually just a matter of tracing things such as charge slips or telephone calls. Fortunately for me most people don't realize how much of their lives are on record somewhere.

However, if X was one of those people who did know, it was very possible he was responsible for Johnson's death, and Martha's disappearance.

It wasn't a comfortable thought to go to sleep with.

THREE

I FELT MUCH BETTER when I woke up the next morning, but by the time I had been poked, prodded, and tested for everything known to man, I didn't feel half as well.

The morning did bring one good thing though, the news that Martha had been found. Sam called to tell me a state trooper had found her about 5:00 a.m. walking along a back road north of Marysville. She was dazed and bruised—presumably from the battle she had put up when she was carried out of the office—and exhausted, but she was otherwise unhurt. The trooper took her to the closest hospital, where they expected to keep her at least overnight.

I was so glad to hear Martha was all right I didn't even complain when it got to be four o'clock in the afternoon before the doctor finally decided it was safe to let me go home.

I was dressed. I had called my cleaning lady, Nora, and asked her to bring me some clothes, plus a silk turban for my head. The ash-brown suit and cream-colored blouse she had chosen didn't do a lot for my looks. I was still pale—actually my skin was a doughy gray—and she had forgotten to bring any makeup, but I was obliged to her for taking the time to bring me the clothes at all, so I didn't complain. I was sitting on the edge of the bed waiting for the nurse to bring my discharge papers when I had another visitor. A young man about the same age as Howie Morgan.

The door was standing open but he stopped in the hall and inquired rather hesitantly if he could talk to me.

"Sure, come on in," I told him. He looked vaguely familiar but I couldn't place him.

"My name is Karl Johnson," he said, coming part way into the room. "It was my father, uh, ah...my father Peter Johnson was the one who, uh... He came to see you about something. I mean, I guess he did."

I pointed at the chair and told him to sit down. He obeyed in such a mechanical way I wondered if he was simpleminded, accustomed to being ordered around. He was an anonymous-appearing man with dull blond hair, faded blue eyes, and a diffident manner. The reason he seemed familiar certainly wasn't because he looked like his father; he reminded me of someone else but I couldn't remember who.

We sat and looked at each other for at least a full minute. I was beginning to think he'd forgotten what he came for when he finally spoke again.

"Do you know who shot my father?" he asked. "Or why they did it?"

He might have been asking what time it was for all the emotion he showed. He was either very stupid, which again seemed possible, or maybe still in shock.

"No, I'm sorry, I don't know a thing about it. I don't even know why he came to see me," I said. His father's story about Karl having an affair with his secretary was obviously ridiculous. I doubted if son Karl was capable of anything anywhere near that enterprising. Which goes to show you how wrong I can be sometimes.

Karl mumbled and stuttered around for a good half hour more while I told him all I knew about the shooting. He thanked me politely and left as hesitantly as he had come, but for all his bumbling ways he managed to extract most of the information I had. I even told him about Martha's kidnapping. I didn't tell him I thought his father had been shot accidentally, nor about his father's demand for a wiretap, and again I don't know why I kept hoarding that bit of the story.

Sam arrived a few minutes after Karl left. He

had called earlier and told me he would pick me up and take me out to dinner if I felt well enough. I did.

I was touched by the concern in his voice when he asked how I was feeling, but mainly I wanted to know what he had found out about Johnson. I like going out with Sam anyway. He is a little old for me, for a date I mean, but he doesn't look or act his age. He will be forty-six his next birthday, and I'm still on the bright side of the big 4-0. Sam is darn good-looking, a kind of combination Paul Newman/Robert Redford, but with dark hair and dimples. I like the way he dresses too, casual, but still sharp. Tonight he was wearing dark-green Dockers with a brown, hand-knit sweater over an olive-green shirt.

It's hard to guess in advance what Sam will tell me about a case he's on. Sometimes he's so close-mouthed you'd think he suspected me of being the perp, but other times he tells me all about it. Sometimes more than I want to know, especially if the case involves a child. This situation was different, though. I was the one who'd been shot, and Martha not only worked for me, she had been kidnapped straight out of my office.

Sam told me about Martha as soon as he came in. He knew I was worried. Unfortunately he hadn't learned anything at all from her, the doctor refused to let him talk to her, and he hadn't gotten much from the medical staff either. She had been taken to ICU because of a heart murmur I was sure she didn't even know she had, and would be kept there at least another twenty-four hours.

Her abduction—if it was that—seemed to have been well planned. It had certainly been accomplished without a hitch. Although actually, as Sam said, we didn't know that she really had been kidnapped. She had not told the state trooper anything except her name and there hadn't been any demands from anyone, so until Sam could talk to Martha he couldn't be sure of anything. Actually the only reason we had for believing she had been kidnapped was that we knew she would not have left the office voluntarily at that time.

We kicked it back and forth all the way down Pill Hill—the locals' name for First Hill, where several large hospitals are located—and across town to the waterfront without coming to any conclusions. Of course, we were looking at it from different angles. He didn't think the two crimes were connected. I was sure they were. Plus I wasn't convinced Johnson was the target; it could just as well have been me the rifleman had in his sights.

Sam took me to Ivar's Restaurant on the docks for fresh salmon steak. Which was especially nice of him, as he doesn't care much for seafood. I can eat it every day of the week.

It was about six-thirty when we got there, and for early July, pleasantly warm. Seattle doesn't normally have any really hot weather until August, but the evening was mild enough to eat outside at one of the dockside tables where I could watch the gulls swooping and swirling over the water. I love gulls. They are so incredibly graceful. I even like their raucous screaming as they fight over the food scraps the tourists throw them.

During dinner Sam told me what he had found out about Peter Johnson's business. So far none of it seemed to have anything to do with his death, but you never know what small fact will turn out to be vital. Actually, I wasn't all that interested in his background, but I did pay attention. I've been wrong before.

"Johnson owns a wholesale restaurant supply outfit," Sam said. "It's called the Great Western Supply Company."

I frowned, trying to remember. "I think I've seen it. Down by the Southcenter Mall some-where."

"Yeah. The office and warehouses are between Renton and Tukwila. You can see the buildings from the freeway."

"Warehouses? Plural?"

"Yes, it's a big operation. He has two warehouses here, plus nine more warehouses, or supply depots, in Texas, New Mexico, and Arizona. Also a fleet of trucks, including six eighteen-wheelers. I haven't dug into that part of it much but apparently his company services a lot of small towns scattered all over the southwest. Towns that aren't big enough to support a wholesaler on their own. Towns that are a long way apart. Seems a lot of restaurant suppliers in that part of the country work that way. They carry a selection of their merchandise on the truck and have a regular route, calling on each customer once or twice a week. Johnson carried mostly dry stock. Flour, sugar, spices, tea, coffee, and those little packets of things restaurants use like mustard and catsup."

"Did he operate the same way around here?" I asked.

"More or less."

"I suppose you've interviewed his office staff and so forth."

"Yeah."

"Well? What did they have to say? What did you find out?"

"So far, not much. We have the basics; he's married and has one son—"

"Oh, I nearly forgot," I interrupted. "His son came to the hospital to see me this afternoon."

Sam gave me a surprised look. "He did? I wasn't too sure he even understood his father was dead. I halfway wondered if he wasn't one slug short of a full load. What did he want?"

I thought a minute. "I'm not sure what he wanted. He asked if I'd seen who did the shooting, and if I knew why he'd been shot, but now that I think about it I have an idea his real purpose was to find out what his father wanted me to do. How old is he? The son, Karl?"

"Twenty-eight. The same as Howie. As a matter of fact, Howie knows him. He met him when he was in school in Texas."

I wondered why Howie hadn't mentioned that to me. "How about his wife?" I asked. "Peter Johnson's wife. Have you talked to her?"

"No. She's not here. She's somewhere in Europe on a trip. Johnson's secretary is trying to locate her."

"Did you talk to her, the secretary?" I'd been

trying to work her into the conversation for the last fifteen minutes. "What does she look like?"

Sam shrugged. "Brunette, about five-four, one hundred twenty pounds, approximately thirty years old."

I could have kicked him. That description could fit half the women in Seattle, but I was afraid to press him for more. Sam was sharp. If he sensed I had any special interest in the secretary he'd start looking for reasons, and I still wanted to keep Johnson's desire for a telephone tap to myself.

The sun had disappeared behind the saw-toothed line of the Olympic Mountains and it was beginning to get cool when we left the restaurant. A violet afterglow made the old red brick buildings across from the docks shimmer with color. Sam had parked in front of a two-story warehouse whose dirt-encrusted windows shone for the moment like pure gold.

We were getting in the car when Sam's pager sputtered to life. He used the car radio to call in.

"There's a homicide in an alley between First and Occidental south of Jackson," the dispatcher told him. "Captain H says it's yours."

Sam muttered something derogatory about the captain's parentage, and backed the car out into the street.

FOUR

SAM DIDN'T HAVE any problem finding the location. There were eight official vehicles and at least twenty men congregated in the short alley where the body had been found. It was in one of the old sections of Seattle near the King Dome. It's a busy area during the day, but dark and deserted at night.

The victim appeared to be a teenage boy. His crumpled body, lying almost dead center in the alley, looked oddly flat and somehow lonely despite the number of people surrounding it. The flashing red light on the ambulance parked near him washed across his face at regular intervals, turning his blood-smeared features an ugly magenta color. His hair, shorter than usual for someone his age, was matted with some greasy substance that was also smeared all over the front of his T-shirt. Both his feet were bare, blood-spattered, and filthy dirty.

He didn't look real either, which was good, as dead bodies are not my thing.

I saw that much before Sam made me move back. Actually, he told me to go wait in the car, but I don't think he expected me to do it. At any rate, I walked back down the alley a bit and stayed there where I could still see and hear.

Across from me and closer to the body, a tall man in a pair of worn Levi's, boots, and a western hat was leaning against a utility pole smoking a thin cigar. He looked like the character Dennis Weaver played in that old TV show *McCloud.* He didn't seem to belong and I wondered what he was doing there.

"I think it happened up that way, Lieutenant," I heard a heavyset man tell Sam, pointing at the far end of the alley. "A bunch of empty crates are strewn around and there's a big drum of some kind of grease dumped over. Probably the same stuff that's smeared on his clothes and in his hair."

Somebody asked Sam if he knew the victim.

"Yeah, his name is Deke Long," Sam said. "In fact, I talked to him this morning. He's no boy, though. He's older than he looks. A lot older. He's twenty-seven, twenty-eight, something like that. Got a rap sheet going back to when he was a kid. He did some time in Walla Walla for a robbery assault, but his parole officer says he's been straight for over a year. Funny." He shook his head.

The man kneeling beside the body got up and called to the medics to bring the stretcher over. I recognized him as Dr. Hazen from the medical examiner's office.

"Are you through?" Sam asked him.

"I guess," he said, looking up with a surprised expression.

"Well?"

"Well, what?" the doctor asked irritably. "What are you so antsy about? I don't know specifically what killed him if that's what you're asking, but he's definitely dead. He was hit on the head with the usual blunt instrument. Hit hard. His scalp is split to the bone. That's where most of the blood came from. He also has a knife slash in his groin, one in his side, and one in his back, any one of which might have killed him. Or he could have been scared to death. I won't know till we do the lab work."

Scowling, Sam glanced at his watch. "How about the time?"

"Unless somebody did something fancy I'd say an hour to an hour and a half, maybe less. Why? Is time important?"

"I don't know. I think..." Sam's voice trailed off into a murmur.

"Well, that's *your* problem," Hazen said. "You're the detective. I'm just the medical examiner. I'll give it to you as close as I can, when I can."

Sam turned as one of the uniformed men came up to him and handed him a plastic evidence bag. The bag contained what looked like a big hunting knife.

"Where did you find it?" Sam asked, holding the sack up to the light.

"Down at the end of the alley almost on the sidewalk."

"You found it? What's your name?"

"Paul Richards. Yeah, me and my partner, Joe Crane, found it, and the body."

"You found the body and went looking for the weapon?" Sam asked, somewhat sharp. Searching a crime scene is not for uniformed patrolmen.

"No, the other way around. The knife caught the light as we came around the corner—it's so big—so we stopped to check it out. Saw the body when we turned into the alley. I went down along the side here and checked him for a pulse while Joe called in."

"Did you see anyone on the street near the alley?"

"Him." Paul gestured at the man in the western outfit who was still standing across from me. "He was down on the next corner, heading up toward Pioneer Square.''

Sam walked over and asked the man something. They had their backs to me and there was a lot of noise up by Long's body, so I couldn't hear what they said, but I saw the man take an identification folder out of his pocket and open it. They shook hands and talked for a moment and then went over to the ambulance. The paramedics had put Long in a body bag and were just starting to roll the stretcher inside.

By that time I was beginning to feel pretty rocky so I went back to Sam's car and curled up on the passenger side of the front seat. I wished I had some aspirin but even without it I was dozing when Sam opened the door.

"Demary, sorry to wake you but I want you to talk to someone," he said, nudging my shoulder.

"I wasn't asleep."

"Good. This is Deputy Sheriff Cass Feliciano from Presidio County, Texas. Sheriff, Demary Jones."

I straightened my turban and gave him a quick once-over. Close up he still reminded me of Dennis Weaver but he was younger and better looking.

"Miss Jones." He nodded and shook my proffered hand. "I asked Lieutenant Morgan if I could

hear your story firsthand but maybe we'd do better
to postpone it till tomorrow. You look pretty tuck-
ered.''

He had a Texas accent that went on forever, and
a smile that turned me into Jell-O. ''I look worse
than I feel,'' I assured him. Which probably wasn't
the truth but I wasn't about to let him get away
too easily. ''What part of my life story are you
interested in?''

''The part where you met Peter Johnson.''

I gave him the same version I had given everyone else and then asked him why he was interested
in Johnson.

''I wasn't interested in Johnson himself up to a
few minutes ago, but now I'm beginning to wonder
if I've been wrong.'' He stopped and looked at his
watch. ''It's only eight-thirty and if you really
don't feel too bad we could go somewhere for a
cup of coffee and I'll tell you all about it. Could
be we have different ends of the same string.''

Sam had to decline, which suited me fine, and
after agreeing to meet with him the following day,
Cass walked me to a rented Cadillac and we
headed back toward my neighborhood where there
are a couple of good coffeehouses.

FIVE

IT TOOK US the better part of an hour to get to my end of town, find a place to park, and get settled in a booth at Café Koffee. I hoped the double-strength latte I ordered would jar me awake because by that time I wasn't feeling too lively.

Cass's story was fairly simple but he didn't tell it well. Or maybe I was just too fuzzy-headed to take it in. Whatever it was, I had a hard time following him.

Cass worked out of a small town, Valentine, southeast of El Paso, and as he said, the biggest part of his arrests had always been drunken drivers or whooping-it-up cowboys. Then, last month, a young local, Leroy Gayland, had been found dead in an arroyo north of town.

"The kid had been shot. He'd been dead for at least forty-eight hours, but other than the fact that he had been dumped there, rather than killed in the arroyo, there wasn't a durn thing to show what happened, or why. Then, a week later, there was another shooting and this time a witness saw a truck leaving the scene."

"What kind of a truck?" Good-looking as this guy was, I didn't know him and I wasn't about to give any information away. I didn't know how much Sam had told him either, so I was trying to be careful what I said, or asked.

"A wholesale freighter out of Albuquerque. The witness, a weekend prospector, found the body while it was still warm. He had a CB in his pickup so he called the state patrol, and they eventually called us in. The victim was again a local kid. Billy Joe Conners. The second killing was pretty much like the first except for one thing. The lab in El Paso found traces of high-grade cocaine in the creases of the guy's hands."

"Somehow you've lost me. What did the truck have to do with finding the body? And where was it? The body, I mean?"

"In a gully about fifty yards off Highway 285."

I must have looked bewildered. I was. "How did—"

Cass interrupted me, laughing. "I'm not making sense to you at all, am I?"

"Not really. I still don't understand what the truck had to do with anything."

"I guess you have to know the country. Right along there, where the body was found, the land is broken up some with runoff gullies and arroyos but on the whole you can see for miles in any direction. So when this ol' boy, the prospector, spotted a truck stopped alongside the road he thought he'd amble on down and see if the driver needed any help. He was on an oil road off to the east and about a half mile away. When he got over to the highway, though, the truck was moving again and was already on down the road a piece. Then, a few minutes later, he found the body.''

I shook my head, and immediately wished I'd had better sense. It felt like I'd pulled ten stitches loose and the doctor had only put in three.

Cass stretched his long legs out into the aisle between the tables and gave me an inquiring look.

''Actually, if I understand you, the prospector doesn't know that the truck driver had anything to do with it at all,'' I said.

''That's about it. And while the driver admitted being on the road at that time, he maintains he was simply traveling his route and had only stopped for a minute to take off his shirt. He said he never got out of the cab at all.''

''I suppose you checked him out for priors?''

''Sure. He's clean. And there wasn't really any reason to suspect him of anything anyway. I did keep thinking about him, though, and the truck. Drugs are always a problem on the border. My area has less trouble than most because we aren't on a direct route to anywhere and you can't even cross

the border near us except on foot or horseback.
There aren't any roads into Mexico and the Sierra
Vieja mountains are a natural barrier. The more I
thought about that truck, though, the more it interested me. 'Specially when I found out the two
boys, Leroy and Billy Joe, had both been working
at the Chuckhouse.''

I frowned. ''You lost me again. What's the
chuckhouse and what does it have to do with anything?''

''The Chuckhouse is a local beanery and the
truck the witness saw was one of Johnson's Great
Western Supply trucks. That same truck had made
a delivery to the Chuckhouse two hours before
Billy Joe's body was found.''

''Was he working at the time?''

''No, and that bothered me until I discovered
that his car had been found at the end of the alley
behind the restaurant.''

''You think he saw, or knew, something about
the first killing and when he jumped the driver he
got himself killed?''

''Almost. What I think is that he got caught
searching the truck.''

''What for? You think the truck was carrying
cocaine? Because of the cocaine on his hands?''

''No. Actually I haven't been able to figure out
the cocaine angle at all. No, I think he had come

to the same faulty conclusion I had and was searching the truck for something that would tie it to Leroy's death. And also because of the way he had been acting the last few days before he was killed. I talked to everyone who knew the two boys, which in a small town in Texas is almost the entire population, and they all said the same thing. Billy Joe had been upset over Leroy's death but he'd also been stirred up over something else. Then, Thursday morning, he told two of his buddies he was on to something big, something worth a lot of money, and that he was goin' to quit his job."

"Maybe he was scared rather than excited."

"Possibly, but I don't think so. Leroy was killed on a Thursday, the same day Johnson's truck made its once-a-week delivery. The followin' Thursday, Billy Joe got himself killed and Johnson's truck was seen leaving the scene."

I took a sip of my latte. I don't really like the stuff and don't know why I keep ordering it. "Do you have any hard evidence?" I asked finally. He had a lot of circumstantial possibilities but so far he hadn't convinced me of anything, except maybe that Johnson really had been the target, not I. Wishful thinking.

"Not a shred. I couldn't even talk ol' Judge Collins into letting me have a warrant to search the truck."

"Probably wouldn't have done you any good anyway. Just warned them off. They would have had plenty of time to steam clean the thing. *If* the truck had anything to do with the murders to start with. So what happened after that? All this was when? Six weeks ago?"

"Right. And you're right, I didn't have anything on Great Western Supply except that one of their trucks happened to be in the vicinity when a body was found and they had made a delivery to the Chuckhouse on each of the two Thursdays in question. But so had three other supply trucks. So I had reason enough to think about the outfit but nothing else until last Monday."

I raised my eyebrows, trying to look intelligent. My head was beginning to hurt so bad I couldn't think straight. Plus, his looks kept distracting me; he had gorgeous blue eyes. They were a turquoise color, surrounded by spiky black lashes no man has the right to have. Every time I looked at him I lost track of what he was talking about.

He took a swallow of his coffee. "Last Monday Peter Johnson called me and wanted to know why I had been investigating his company."

SIX

MARTHA CALLED ME from her apartment at eleven the next morning. I was immensely relieved to hear her buttery-smooth voice with its broad English accent. The doctor had released her early, and Sam had gone himself to get her.

"I feel bloody awful but I'm all right," she assured me. "How about yourself? Sam said they let you out last evening."

"I'm fine," I told her. "I still have a headache but it isn't too bad. What about the heart murmur?"

"I don't have one. The doctor decided it was just a reaction to being snatched. Stress-related atrial fibrillation. I was more tired than anything else. The sods who dragged me out of the office left me tied to a tree out in the bushes somewhere. It took me hours to work myself free."

"Well, lie around for a day or so. That's what *I'm* going to do. My doctor told me to take it easy and for once I think I'll do what I'm told. I'm going to have some Chinese sent in this evening.

Why don't you and Charles come over and we'll compare stories?''

Martha and I don't socialize much as a rule. She has a permanent man in her life, which I don't, plus most of her friends are university people, but this was different.

''All right. I'm not sure Charles can make it but I'll be over around six,'' she said.

We exchanged a few more words and then hung up.

Charles Kingman is Martha's husband. He's a professor at the University of Washington. They met at Berkeley ten years ago when Charles was working on his doctorate and she was an undergraduate. Martha wouldn't marry him for a long time; she didn't think marriage would work because she never got her degree. In some ways she is guilty of reverse snobbery.

Personally, I don't think Charles cares one way or the other. I guess he is good in his field, medieval English literature, but most of the time he doesn't even seem to know what day it is, let alone what letters Martha doesn't have after her name. I have often wondered if he even realizes that she is so beautiful. He has the personality of an oatmeal cookie. I never have been able to figure out what she sees in him.

Thinking about him brought Karl Johnson to my mind and I realized he was who Karl reminded me of. They didn't look anything alike but they both had the same vague manner, as if they came from another dimension and would soon be on their way back to whatever space they normally inhabited.

The doctor had told me to lay off coffee for a couple of days. I had forgotten that last night, to my sorrow, so after Martha called I went up to the kitchen and fixed myself a pot of herb tea before I went back to the notes I'd been working on.

I own a really super house. It was my great-aunt's. She left it to me in her will. She didn't have any children and all her siblings were gone before her. A horrendous mortgage went with the house so actually the bank and I are joint owners, but I'm gradually gaining on them. The place looks like a Victorian wedding cake. Tall and narrow—it's only forty-five feet wide including the wraparound porches on all three floors—with acres of gingerbread trim, scalloped and diamond-shaped shingles, fancy carved window valances, and elaborately turned railings on the porches. Inside, all the rooms have ten-foot ceilings with ornate plastered corners, and hardwood plank floors. There are three bedrooms, five fireplaces, and a kitchen the size of a skating rink. It does have a couple of

disadvantages, though. There is only one bathroom, and for some unknown reason the kitchen
and dining room are on the second floor.

So I went upstairs and fixed myself a pot of
chamomile tea and then went back down to what
was originally the library to work on my notes.

I have an IBM 386 at home and while I didn't
have much on the Johnson case yet, I wanted to
get what I did know into the computer before I
forgot anything.

I still had some reservations but Cass Feliciano's
story had me pretty well convinced that Peter Johnson had been the target.

Johnson had called Cass on Monday morning,
not to complain, but to ask why Cass thought Great
Western Supply was involved in anything illegal.

Apparently they had both done considerable
beating around the bush but in the end Johnson had
offered to pay Cass's airfare to Seattle if he would
come up and talk face-to-face. He had not told him
what he wanted to talk about, nor had he given
Cass any information, but as he was willing to foot
the bill Cass's boss had told him to go. He had
arrived at Seatac International approximately an
hour after Johnson had been shot in my doorway.

As per their telephone arrangements, Cass had
hired a car and driven to Johnson's office. He was

at Great Western, still waiting, when the police called with the news of Johnson's death. In the resulting confusion he had managed to spend an hour or more talking to people without being questioned about his right to be there. He said he hadn't really learned anything but he had picked up some interesting impressions.

One, Johnson seemed to be both respected and liked as a boss, which contradicted my impression of him. And two, son Karl was also liked, although, like myself, Cass thought him pretty much of a dimwit. Cass was also told that father and son got along well. That didn't fit my impression either.

I didn't tell Cass about Johnson wanting a wiretap but I did manage to work the conversation around to Johnson's secretary. And for the second time it didn't do me any good. He hadn't seen her at all, or at any rate he hadn't seen anyone who identified herself as such.

I did tell Martha about the wiretap that evening. She arrived early and alone.

"Charles is conducting a seminar this evening," she said as she came in. "He may be over later, though. He said he wants to talk to you."

I gave her a questioning look. "What about?"

"I have no idea." She grimaced as she took off

her coat. "Those sods tied my arms behind me and I not only pulled a shoulder muscle trying to get loose, my whole back hurts."

"Here, give me your coat. Do you want a drink? A glass of wine?" I tossed her coat at the hall tree and followed her into the front room. It's a fairly large room with uncurtained windows on two sides. They are high and narrow with fanlights of leaded glass above the lintels. Folding shutters painted a creamy off-white serve in place of drapes.

"No, nothing alcoholic," she said. "I'm full of painkillers. I'll have tea later." She sank onto one of the two silk upholstered love seats I have facing each other in front of the fireplace. "I'm anxious to hear what happened to you."

"To me?" I stared at her, surprised. "You must have seen more than I did. I didn't see anyone but Johnson."

"You mean that's all? But I thought... From what Sam Morgan said I thought you knew all about it."

I laughed. "What a sneak he is. I wondered why he went up there and got you himself instead of sending someone. He wanted to talk to you before we had a chance to compare notes."

Martha scowled. "That man is paranoid. He

doesn't trust anybody. And a fat lot of good it does him. In this case, I felt too lousy to talk at all, but as it happens I don't know dickey-bird about anything anyway.''

"You know more than I do," I told her. "The last I remember I heard this thunderclap in my head and you were screaming. So, go on from there."

"Unfortunately there isn't much I can add. After I showed Peter Johnson into your office I went around to the stockroom where I keep the back files to see if I could find the Winston folder. I've misplaced it somewhere and she wants copies of those family-tree charts you did for her. I think I was in there about five minutes before I found it and started back out front. I didn't hear anyone or anything at all but as I came out of the doorway someone grabbed me around the neck from behind. I stomped on his instep and tried to twist away from him but a second one got an arm around my waist and another grabbed my wrists. Then they started marching me down the hall.''

"Did you see what they looked like?''

"No, not really. It happened too fast. I know there were three of them to start with, and that they were all black and all big. They were all taller than

I am by several inches, which would put them well over six feet.''

"You're sure they were black?''

"Positive. I did see bits and pieces of them while we were struggling in the hall, and I saw their hands again when they tied me to the blasted tree. I told Sam all this but one thing I didn't tell him was I think they are members of the street gang that has been terrorizing shop owners in the south end. The ones who call themselves the New Janizarys.''

"What makes you think it's them?'' I asked, frowning at her. "And why didn't you tell Sam?''

"Because I don't know why I think so and I didn't want him nattering away at me all morning. I will let him know if it comes to me, but at the moment I simply don't remember what ticked me. It must be something they said or did but I can't put my finger on it now. Nothing to do with what they looked like at any rate, because I didn't see them. But to get back to Tuesday, I did some kicking and struggling as they dragged me down the hall but I couldn't yell because the one behind me with his arm around my neck was holding a dirty rag of some kind over my mouth and most of my face. Which was another reason I saw so little.''

"How long did all of this take? Can you make a guess?"

"Two minutes maybe? No more than that, and probably less. Then, just as I heard the front door open and heard you say something, I got the one behind me in the kneecap with my heel. He let go of my face, I screamed, I heard the shots, and that was it. Somebody hit me and I was out of it." She fingered her jaw tenderly. The purple bruise marred her beautiful chocolate skin. "The next thing I remember is waking up in the van."

"When? Do you know how long it was after they grabbed you?"

"Not the foggiest. I woke up facedown, bound, gagged, and blindfolded, lying on some kind of a filthy mat with a canvas over me. I tried to get out from under the thing, believe me I tried, but I was trussed up like a Christmas turkey. I simply couldn't move, and it was so airless under there I thought I would suffocate."

"Canvas? Not a blanket?"

"No, it was something heavy." She shuddered and put her hand over her face for a moment. "I really thought I'd bought the farm," she said thickly, using an old Vietnam War expression.

I didn't say anything and in a minute she took a deep breath and went on.

"I don't know how long they left me there. It seemed like forever but it may not have been more than an hour or so. Eventually they came back. Several men this time."

"How many is several?"

"I don't know, but I heard, or could distinguish, at least four voices and I think possibly five. They pulled the canvas back and took a look at me, then two of them got in front and we drove off. I guess they didn't pull the cover back over me as tight as it had been because from then on I could breathe better, and I could hear their voices a little. I couldn't hear words, though. I don't know if the two that drove the van were part of the original three or not because I didn't really see any of them and I didn't hear the first three say anything."

I was starting to ask her what the second two had to say when I was interrupted by the doorbell. The delivery boy from the Half Moon Café had arrived.

I had told the old man who owns the place, Mr. Choom, to send enough for three people but I hadn't asked for any particular dishes. He sent a regular banquet. We had two different kinds of shrimp, chicken chow yuk, moo goo gai pan, glazed lobster in a sweet-and-sour sauce, pork fried rice, and two other containers of stuff I couldn't even name.

We had to carry it upstairs but the table was already set in front of the windows that overlook the backyard. I like the table there so I can look out and see the little fish pond in the middle.

I'm not a gardener; in fact, I hate grubbing around in the dirt, so the yard is mostly tile with a few ornamental trees in big pottery tubs. It's all enclosed by a high board fence. In the spring Nora helps me hang flower baskets on all the fence posts but that's about the extent of what I do outside. There are a couple of raised flower beds that Nora weeds once in a while. She is one of that rare breed of cleaning ladies who likes the outside of the house to be as tidy as the inside.

Martha and I ate until we were stuffed.

Afterward I filled her in on everything I knew, and she finished telling me her story. The last half was no more informative than the first part.

She said they drove for quite a while and after they stopped they left her in the van for another long time before they pulled her out and walked her up a small rise and tied her to the tree.

I rubbed my head through the paisley silk turban I'd put on. I looked so weird—half bald like that—

I couldn't bear to see myself, let alone have anyone else see me.

"Didn't you see or hear anything that would help identify them, Martha? Or anything that gives you any idea why they grabbed you in the first place?"

"Demary, I didn't see anything ever, except what I told you. They never took the blindfold off and none of them ever said anything to me, or more than one or two words to each other. Things like 'turn right' or 'slow down.' Just after they tied me to the tree I did hear one of them say something about getting on the wrong road, but that's it. They were either being very careful that I didn't hear their voices or they were communicating by sign language."

"Darn," I muttered. "There just isn't anything to get a handle on."

Martha sighed. "I'm going home," she said abruptly. "I feel simply filthy and you don't look any better than I feel. Go to bed. If Charles shows up don't answer the door."

I didn't argue. Bed sounded good. Charles didn't come and I never did find out what he wanted either. The next time I saw him he had forgotten that he even intended to come to my house.

SEVEN

I DIDN'T OPEN THE OFFICE Friday but I did go in. I spent an hour or so trying to establish a connection between X and the New Janizary gang, or X and Peter Johnson, made several calls, and checked all the files. I was reasonably sure there were no connections to find, but I needed to be certain. I wasn't happy. I was mad, and scared, and furious about Johnson being shot right in my office, and I intended to do something about it. I'd never before witnessed a murder, or been directly involved in a homicide investigation. So before I started snooping I wanted to know whose toes I might step on. I didn't think finding a missing murderer would be any more difficult than finding an obscure ancestor, or for that matter, any other missing person, but it never hurt to be cautious. It turned out I was wrong about the difficulties, but that was the thought I started with.

I also called and got a one o'clock appointment with Ruth, the woman who cuts my hair, then set up a meeting with Karl Johnson at his father's office for four o'clock.

Ruth took one look at me with my turban off and started to laugh so hard I thought she was going make herself ill. I was ticked off for a minute, but after looking at myself in her big mirrors I had to laugh too. I really was a sight. And, as she said, there was absolutely nothing that could be done about it except shave the rest of my head and use a wig until my hair grew out again.

We tried a variety. It was kind of fun seeing what I'd look like—as a sugar blond (not bad), as a brunet (awful)—but in the end she found a wig that looked so much like my own red mop no one ever noticed I had one on. It even complemented my green eyes.

I was out of her place by quarter of two. I got in my car, a beat-up old Toyota Corona that never misses a stroke, and took Interstate 5 to where I could turn off and pick up the road to Johnson's warehouse. For a change there wasn't much traffic. When I took the off-ramp at Southcenter I had a good forty-five minutes to spare. I used them in the shopping mall buying myself a new Liz Claiborne outfit in shades of bronze and green. I deserved a treat after what I'd been through. It isn't every day you see yourself with a naked skull.

The warehouses and office of the Great Western Supply Company are in one of the new industrial complexes that are slowly turning the Green River valley into a concrete wasteland.

The main office was on the second floor and was about as palatial as a barn. The reception room had worn linoleum floor covering, two plastic chairs for visitors, and a battered wooden desk for the receptionist that looked like it might have seen the light of day in a World War II army orderly room. What I could see of the individual offices looked much the same, including Johnson's, to which I was shown immediately. But every desk was equipped with a big IBM terminal, there were fax machines, laser printers, and several of the newest Canon copiers in sight, and the communication system was top-of-the-line. Peter Johnson had obviously believed in spending his money where it would do him the most good, not on show.

Karl met me at the office door and invited me in, pointing toward another plastic chair in front of the desk.

"I'm sorry I can't offer you anything better," he said, giving the chair a troubled look. "My father didn't believe in..." His voice trailed off into a mumble, then strengthened purposefully. "I'm planning to have the offices done over as soon as possible."

"Is Great Western a family-owned concern?" I

asked, lowering myself gingerly. The seat didn't look any too secure.

"Family? Oh. You mean do we, uh, yes.... Well, yes. That is, my father owned it, or I guess in this state it would be my father and mother. My mother will own it now. I think." He gave me a puzzled look. "Why?"

"Why, what?" I asked, trying to match his off-beat manner.

"Why do you want to know?"

"I just wondered. Somebody shot him. I wondered who profited."

He smiled. He had a nice smile. "A motive? Yes, I guess owning the company would be a motive but my mother doesn't need the money, and she wasn't here anyway. Miss Wagoner finally located her last night. She was in Rome."

"How about you?" I asked, wondering how far I could go before he told me to kiss off. The question didn't seem to bother him, though.

Frowning, he told me that he loved his father and didn't have any reason to kill him. He had ample money of his own. His maternal grandparents had been very wealthy and had left both him and his mother a sizeable fortune each.

"That wasn't what I meant," I said. "I wondered where you were when your father was shot."

"Oh. I was at the Crescent Company on Dearborn Street. You can check with Lieutenant Morgan; he already asked me. And I'm sure he must have confirmed it with someone there."

There were several more things I wanted to know but talking to Karl was much like chatting with one of those voice-activated computers. He answered, and as far as I could tell without any particular hesitation, but there wasn't much life to the conversation. Actually, it wasn't a conversation. He answered my questions in his vague bumbling way, but he didn't volunteer anything, or ask anything. He had apparently satisfied his own curiosity yesterday and wasn't particularly interested in hearing anything more. At least nothing I might have to say.

He did have one query as I got up to leave. "Are you investigating my father's murder?" he asked. "Has someone hired you?"

"No, no one has hired me. But he was killed leaving my office and I don't care much for that. Makes me mad. I got shot too, and I don't like that either. I want to know who did it." I was still trying to match Karl's laid-back manner, but it didn't come out quite right. The words were okay but there was a sharp edge to my voice.

"If you aren't careful somebody might shoot you again," he said as he opened the door.

I gaped at him. Coming from anyone else I would have considered the words a definite threat, but the way he said it I couldn't be sure. He apparently recognized that at the same time.

"No. That isn't what...I mean, uh...I mean..." He gave up and looked at me with a worried frown.

"Never mind," I told him. "You mean I should be careful, and I will." I stuck out my hand. "Thanks for talking to me."

He gave my hand a limp shake and motioned at a woman coming down the hall. "She'll take care of you."

I didn't know that I needed anyone to take care of me but I followed her down the hall. The lady did not precisely match Sam's description—for one thing, she was closer to forty than she was to thirty—but I took a chance. "I hope Mr. Johnson's death has not disrupted the company completely, Miss Wagoner," I said sweetly, giving her my number-two silly giggle. "It's so hard for a lone female to keep things going smoothly."

She flicked me a sideways glance without answering. Women are harder to fool than men. I was about to try something else when she took me by the arm and steered me past the receptionist with a hissed admonition to shut up. We were out the door and halfway to the elevators before I got over my surprise.

"Sorry. I don't want anyone to see me talking to you so just follow my lead, please," she said sharply. Dropping my arm, she punched the elevator button and moved several feet away from me.

There wasn't a soul in sight but I decided I'd better not mention that. I was anxious to hear what she had to say, whatever it was, and she looked like she might walk off and leave me flat if I didn't follow orders.

The two men already in the elevator when it stopped eyed me curiously. Miss Wagoner ignored them, got out on the ground floor, and strode toward the exit. I followed at a trot. At the first crosshall she glanced behind us, then motioned me toward a doorway on our right. It led to a women's rest room as Spartan as the rest of the place.

She checked the stalls before turning back to me. "I'm sorry to be so melodramatic," she said, eyeing me calmly. "I was going to call you but this seemed like too good an opportunity to miss. I still don't want anyone to know I've talked to you, though."

"Why not? Do you think someone in the company here is responsible for Peter Johnson's death?'' That was an interesting thought.

She hesitated, giving me an odd look. "Do you have any ID?''

I dug my PI license out of my purse. It's better than a driver's license for identification, so I still carry it. I suppose I should have told her right then that having the license didn't mean anything. As I had told her boss, I'm a researcher, not a private investigator. Whatever that really is. However, for better or worse, I didn't.

She checked the license over thoroughly before handing it back. "Your looks don't match your reputation,'' she said. "I called a man I know in the public defender's office. He said you were good. Frankly, you don't look like you even have good sense.''

I grinned. "Thanks a whole big bunch, Miss Wagoner'' I said, wondering who in the world she had talked to.

"I'm sorry.'' She gave an embarrassed little laugh. "I didn't mean that quite like it sounded. And please, call me Helen. But to answer your question, yes, I do think someone in the company might be responsible for Mr. Johnson's death. I don't have any idea who it is, but I'll tell you why I think so.''

I held up my hand to stop her and took a quick look out the door. The hall was empty. "If there is a chance you're on to anything, let's do this right," I told her, turning on the tap in the basin. "The noise of the water will cover your voice."

She nodded and moved over closer to me. "About a month ago Mr. Johnson made a trip to the Albuquerque store and when he came back he had something on his mind, something that really seemed to bother him. I know...knew...him well and I could tell. He didn't get over it either. Then, this last weekend something else happened. I don't know what it was but I do know it had to do with the warehouse because I found out he was over there all night Saturday night, and again Sunday night."

"How do you know that?"

"I took Dave Porter, he's the night watchman, to the airport Monday morning. He was going on vacation, and as we live in the same neighborhood I took him out there so he wouldn't have to leave his car in the parking lot for two weeks. On the way he told me about Mr. Johnson being in the warehouse. He just mentioned it in conversation but I—"

"Wait a minute," I interrupted. "Can you remember exactly what he said?"

She thought a minute. "No, not exactly. We were talking about him, Dave I mean, going on vacation, and he said something about Mr. Johnson needing one too. He said Mr. Johnson worked too hard and was crazy to be taking a manual inventory when it was all on computer. When I asked him what in the world made him think Mr. Johnson was doing an inventory he said he must have been doing one. Why else would he spend all night checking stock?"

"Did he say he actually saw Johnson checking boxes?"

"No. I asked him that. He said he noticed him come in and start walking up and down the aisles, and later saw him in the warehouse office looking at a sheaf of invoices. That was all. He didn't know when he left the building on Saturday night, but did see him leave on Sunday, or actually that morning, Monday morning, at three-thirty."

"Did Johnson say anything to him?"

"I don't know because about then we got to the passenger-loading zone and Dave got out. And of course at the time it was just chitchat. The only reason I paid any attention at all was because I knew something was bothering Mr. Johnson."

"Did you ask him why he was there? Johnson?"

She looked at me as if I had lost my mind. "Of course not. You met him, you must have seen what kind of a man he was."

"Lieutenant Morgan has the idea that he was well liked around here. That he was considered a good boss."

She shrugged. "He was. A good boss, I mean. But that doesn't mean he was friendly, or would allow anyone to question anything he did. I've worked for him for eleven years and I still called him Mr. Johnson, which should tell you something. I liked working for him because he told me exactly what he wanted done and then let me go ahead and do it without any interference. However, that doesn't have anything to do with what I'm telling you."

"There's more?"

She gave me another of those exasperated looks that reminded me of an old-maid schoolteacher I had in the fifth grade.

"I got to the office about forty-five minutes early that morning because of taking Dave to the plane, and when I got here Mr. Johnson was in my office working on the computer. We have a mainframe system that is connected to all the PCs and to the other stores by modem. It is quite complex and I didn't think Mr. Johnson knew enough about it to be using it. By that I mean I didn't want him inadvertently erasing information that would take us hours, or even weeks, to recover. Do you know anything about computers?''

''Yes.''

''Then maybe you can understand my problem at that point. If I interrupted him he'd be furious, and if I didn't he could easily destroy thousands of dollars' worth of work. I was still trying to make up my mind what to do when he shut the whole system down.''

''Accidentally?''

''Yes and no. I think he finished what he was doing, at least he looked like he was done, and I think he may have meant to store or save it. I could see him through the glass door to my office. I'm not sure whether he actually saved the file or not, but I do know he didn't mean to shut the system down. He was thoroughly annoyed because it took the computer operators several hours to catch up on the orders that had come in from New Mexico and Arizona. The order system is automated, and... Well, that isn't the point. At the time he told me good morning and went on back to his own office without any explanation, which I didn't expect anyway. Later on that morning when things smoothed out I checked the automatic log on my hard-drive and saw that he had worked on my terminal for three hours and fifteen minutes. Which meant he must have come straight to the office from the warehouse.''

''Could you tell what he had been working on?''

''No. When he shut everything down he scrambled the tree. The access lines.''

I nodded, thinking. ''Look, Helen,'' I said finally. ''You're going to have to tell Lieutenant Morgan about this.'' As much as I hated to admit it, Morgan was better equipped to deal with this kind of an inquiry than I was.

''No,'' she said sharply. ''You can tell him what I've said if you want to, but I'm not going to talk to the police at all. Not after what happened to that warehouseman.''

''What warehouseman?'' I asked, confused. ''The night watchman?''

''No. That boy. Deke Long. He was seen talking to Lieutenant Morgan Wednesday morning. Karl told me. And someone else saw him, they must have, because that night someone killed him. They stabbed him. No. I'm not going to talk to Lieutenant Morgan.''

EIGHT

MY ANSWERING MACHINE was lit up like a Las Vegas casino when I got home. The little digital number screen said I had received seven calls between noon and 6:10. The clock read 6:18.

I ignored the thing and went on up to the kitchen and made a cup of tea. I was so tired I didn't even want to eat, very unusual for me. It had been a frustrating afternoon and the whack on my head was still taking its toll.

After I left Great Western I called Sam Morgan from the first telephone I could find and arranged to meet him for an early dinner at McRory's in the Pioneer Square district. I meant to tell him about Johnson wanting the wiretap along with telling him about my talk with Miss Wagoner. Instead we got into a flaming row over Deke Long and I stormed out of the place without even ordering.

I was annoyed at Sam for not telling me about Deke Long working at Great Western but actually that wasn't what started the argument. What started it was him telling me to stay out of the Johnson case, to stay away from Great Western, and, in short, to mind my own business.

When I told him I thought my getting shot kind of made it my business, he said I was not a detective, and wasn't qualified to investigate a homicide. Also he didn't want me meddling with his department—or words to that effect.

About then I made a few remarks I shouldn't have and, needless to say, after that he wouldn't tell me anything. I was going to have to let him know what Helen Wagoner had told me about the night watchman, Dave Porter, and do it fairly soon if I didn't want him really mad at me, but I wasn't going to do it that evening. Even if he knew about him, Sam wouldn't bother calling Porter until morning anyway.

I knew he was worried about my getting myself into trouble, and I knew I didn't have the expertise to investigate a murder, but telling me I didn't know what the heck I was doing sure wasn't the way to get me to back off.

And then, to compound my frustration, I hadn't been able to find Joey Winters, my local snitch.

Before we had started sniping at each other, Sam told me they had pinpointed where the shots had come from. The trajectory specialists placed the killer directly across the street from my office in the second-floor hallway of an old apartment building. They had also found where he had stashed the rifle in a jardiniere full of pampas grass. Not the rifle itself, just traces of it having been there. The building was kept locked night and day and there was no intercom system, so unless he was a tenant someone had let him in. He could have picked the lock, of course, although it didn't seem likely considering the time of day. So far, they had not come up with a witness who had seen anything suspicious, but if anyone could sniff out that kind of information it was Joey Winters.

Thirteen-year-old Joey was a favorite of mine. He was a kid who wanted to know about everything that was going on in the neighborhood. He also knew more than he should about the people in the neighborhood. Information he was more than willing to share with me. Sometimes more willing than I wanted. I had gone looking for him on my way home but hadn't had any luck.

Still fuming over Sam's bullheaded attitude, I poured myself a second cup of tea and ate some of the cold Chinese food left from the night before. The meal, such as it was, revived me enough to clean up the kitchen. I knew if I didn't at least get the dishes in the dishwasher I'd hear about it from

Nora. The next day was her morning at my house. She comes half a day every two weeks.

I had inherited Nora, and her sharp tongue, along with the house. Not that she is any kind of old family retainer—she is only a couple of years older than I am, dresses better than I do, and drives a Porsche—she just happened to be working for my great-aunt when the old lady died and after thinking it over she had agreed to give me a try. Believe me, good cleaning women choose their employers, not the other way around.

I had the kitchen done and was reading the paper when I remembered my answering machine and went down to check it. The machine was new to me—I'd had it installed in June—and I wasn't sure I liked it. It appeared easy enough to use but it had turned out to be somewhat tricky and the instrument itself was cumbersome looking. The salesman had talked me into buying it because it included a burglar alarm/police alert system, and living alone in a big house can be scary sometimes.

Two of the calls were from friends asking how I was doing. One was from Martha telling me she was feeling better and would be back in the office on Monday. She, as usual, had stated the time: four o'clock. The next one was from Sam asking me to call him. The following one was Cass Feliciano saying he would try again at seven o'clock. The last was Sam again. He had apparently called the second time between when I left McRory's and when I got home. He said to call him. Immediately!

"Forget you," I told the machine as I hit the erase button.

The bell shrilled back at me, nearly startling me out of my wits.

I jerked the handset off the cradle. "Yes? Who is it?" I asked rudely.

"Cass Feliciano," he said, sounding amused. "Did I call at a bad time?"

His tone was so superior, so male, I nearly slammed the phone in his ear but I caught myself in time. I wasn't going to learn anything from him either if I let my temper get away from me again.

I took a deep breath, grimaced at my reflection in the glass-fronted bookcase across the room, and spoke sweetly. "Of course not. I was waiting to hear from you," I said, giving his ego a stroke. "I thought the call was from someone else."

"How about having dinner with me, then?"

"Now?"

"Sure. Why not? You haven't eaten already, have you?"

"Uh, no, of course not," I lied. "I do have to

make it an early evening though. I'm still feeling
the effects of that wallop on the head." That much
was true, but I also wanted to know if he'd learned
anything new.

"That's all right, we'll just have dinner," he
said. "I'll pick you up in twenty minutes and we'll
eat at that Chinese place near your house, the Half
Moon Café."

I WAS THOROUGHLY TIRED of moo goo gai pan by
the time I finished eating it for the third time in
twenty-four hours, but I was glad I'd agreed to
meet him. I was sorry I felt so rotten, though. It
had been a long time since I'd met a man I liked
as well on short acquaintance as I did Cass Feliciano. He was warm, and funny, he didn't talk
down to me, and he was the most attractive guy
I'd been out with in many a day. He was also willing to share any information he had and the first
thing he told me was that Helen Wagoner had
called Sam Morgan while he was in Sam's office.
I'd given her the number, and warned her she was
taking a big chance by not calling him, but I really
hadn't expected her to do it. I was glad I'd been
wrong. If nothing else it got me off the hook. It
also answered the question of how Sam had known

I'd been out to Great Western. I'd been wondering about that.

Cass answered something else that had been bothering me. Namely, how had Peter Johnson known Cass was interested in Great Western Supply?

"I just found out myself," Cass told me in answer to my question. "I talked to my boss this morning. He told me the Albuquerque office called him yesterday. To make the story short, the sheriff there had just discovered that one of his deputies had told Johnson I was running a check on his employees."

"When?" I asked.

"When what? When did he tell Johnson?"

I nodded. "Yes."

"About a month ago. Right after I was up there, I guess."

"Isn't that kind of unusual? I don't know anything about how a sheriff's office works, I mean in comparison to the local homicide department, but telling a suspect—"

"No one suspected Johnson of anything," Cass interrupted. "Or at least *I* didn't. But, yes, the guy had no business telling Johnson I was checking out Great Western. I guess he is, or was, a personal friend of Johnson's."

"When you were looking around in Albuquerque did you find anything that pointed to Seattle?"

"No. Nothing. As I said, I didn't find anything suspicious at all. They operate in a perfectly ordinary way as far as I could tell, and none of their Albuquerque employees has a record. Until Johnson called me I'd pretty well crossed them off my list as suspects."

"Well, at least we know why Johnson wanted..." I stopped in mid-sentence. I had nearly told him about the wiretap. I was more tired than I realized.

"What did he want?" Cass asked easily. "You never did say."

"I don't know what he wanted me to do," I said, with the emphasis on wanted. "I meant we know why he came to see me."

That pretty well ended the evening. He knew I was lying, and I knew he knew, but at least he didn't hassle me about it. We left a few minutes later, nearly running into Howie Morgan in the doorway.

He stopped us, of course, and wanted to know how I felt. Which, for a minute, sent my temper soaring. I was going to ask him what the heck he thought he was doing following me around, then remembered that this was his precinct. He was simply checking out his beat.

"I'm much better, still a little shaky, but I'll be all right," I told him, doing my best to sound pleasant.

"Have you got a line on the shooter yet?" he asked. "Or any kind of a lead?"

"Not yet." I introduced him to Cass. "This is Sheriff Feliciano from Valentine, Texas. He has a case pending that may have something to do with Johnson's death."

"Oh? How so?"

Cass filled him in, politely, if a bit briefly.

"Other than the Great Western Supply Company itself it doesn't sound as if you have anything that really ties the two cases together," Howie said as Cass finished bringing him up to date.

"True."

"Well, tell me this, Cass, how sure are you that there *is* a connection?" Howie asked, sounding as egotistical as ever.

Irritated, I stomped off and got in the car. Cass followed a moment later.

"I take it Howie isn't one of your favorite people. Mind telling me why not?" Cass asked as we drove away.

"Was I that obvious?" I asked, ashamed of myself. I didn't have anything against Howie, not really, he was just such a pompous jerk. But I'd hate to have my opinion get back to Sam.

"I don't think so. I don't think he noticed anyway," Cass said reassuringly. "He just wanted to know how the investigation was going."

"He rubs me wrong," I told him. "I never have liked him. He's smarmy. Always so polite, so pleasant, to everyone except Sam. Sam thinks he walks on water, and he can't, or won't, see what Howie is really like."

Cass grinned. "Sounds like a perfectly normal father to me."

I sighed. "I guess so."

"Has Howie always been like that, or is this something new?"

"It's not new. He's always been a pain, or at least he has been ever since his mother died. Howie was sixteen when she died and for some reason he blamed Sam for her death, which was stupid because she died from a fall down a flight of stairs while Sam was at work. But from then on he gave Sam a bad time. He never got into any real trouble; he just made Sam miserable every way he could, any time he could. I think things have been better between them since Howie joined the force, though."

"I take it you've known Sam a long time. Did you know his wife too?"

"I met her first," I said shortly, glad my house was just ahead of us. I didn't want to talk about that meeting. I'd met Angie Morgan just the one time, over fifteen years ago. I'd made such a fool of myself it still made me squirm with embarrassment every time I thought about it. I had been very young and I don't think Sam even remembered the meeting, but I did.

Cass walked me to the door, brushed a feather-weight kiss across my mouth, and was back down the steps before I could react. Which was just as well. I wasn't in shape for much more than a kiss. But it might have been fun to try.

NINE

I WAS IN BED, lights out and asleep by ten-thirty.
Tired as I was, however, I woke up wide awake at
three in the morning and couldn't go back to sleep.

I gave up after a while and turned on the light,
deciding that I might as well work up some notes
on the Johnson case. I couldn't concentrate on it,
though. I had Angie Morgan on my mind. I hadn't
thought of Angie in years, and didn't really have
any particular reason for thinking about her then.
What I'd told Cass was the truth, as far as it went,
but what I hadn't told him was that I never really
knew Angie at all. I knew *of* her, which is something different.

The first time I saw her I mistook her for a
hooker. We were both standing on the corner of
First and Pike waiting for the light to change when
Sam, whom I knew by sight, drove up in his patrol
car and told her to get in. I thought he was busting
her and I tried to talk him out of it. When he didn't
respond the way I expected, I got smart-mouthed.
I don't think Angie understood what I was talking
about but of course Sam did. He was actually

pretty good about it. He simply told me to back off and they drove away. I didn't find out she was his wife until much later when I got to know Sam personally.

She died a few years after that in one of those stupid home accidents. She was alone in the house when it happened so there was never any way of telling for sure, but it looked as if she was taking a bath when either the phone or the doorbell rang. She apparently got out of the tub, started downstairs, tripped, and fell. When Sam got home that night he found her at the bottom of the stairs with a broken neck, naked, with her bathrobe tangled around her legs. The tub was still full of tepid, soapy water.

Young Howie was away, staying overnight at a friend's house. Sam didn't know which friend; in fact, he wouldn't have known where Howie was at all if the boy hadn't left his mother a note beside the telephone. Sam didn't want to call around, so Howie didn't learn of his mother's death until he came back the following morning. For some reason he blamed Sam for Angie's death, which was absurd, and he never forgave his father for not locating him that night.

Thinking about the way Howie acted at the time suddenly put an unpleasant thought in my mind. If

Howie hadn't been a sixteen-year-old kid, and the son of a police sergeant—it was before Sam made Lieutenant—his behavior might have raised some questions. However, it had all happened a long time ago, and right now I had something more important to think about.

I propped myself up on some pillows, picked up the clipboard I always keep on my bedside table, then sat looking blankly at the paper. There was something so out of focus about Johnson's death I couldn't get started.

The timing itself was fairly straightforward. Peter Johnson had called my office at ten o'clock on Monday morning and made an appointment for one-thirty the following day. He arrived early—at one-fifteen—and was leaving at one-forty, give or take a minute, when he was shot.

At the same time—one-forty—Martha was overpowered by three intruders and dragged out of the building.

The problem was the two crimes were so totally different in method and execution they didn't fit. It was almost as if they had been carried out by two different sets of people. And the chance of that being true must be something like my chances of winning the state lottery. Astronomical was the word.

The second big question was how had the gunman known Peter Johnson would be at my office
that afternoon? Johnson had made the appointment
himself and, unless he'd told someone, which
didn't seem in character, only two people knew
he'd be there at that time. Johnson himself, and
Martha. I hadn't even known until I checked my
appointments Tuesday morning.

There was always the possibility that his death
was simply the result of a random shooting, but I
didn't believe that. There was also the possibility
that the killer had followed Peter Johnson from
Great Western, but again I didn't think so. Despite
some of the inconsistencies, the shooting had been
too well executed to be a spur-of-the-moment job,
as was Martha's kidnapping. So, if we were looking for one perp, what was the connection between
the two crimes?

Helen Wagoner had told me that my name, and
the time of our appointment, was written on Johnson's day book, but she said she had not seen the
notation until Monday afternoon and he hadn't
mentioned it to her at all. Also, again according to
Helen, no one ever went into Peter J's office except
by invitation, and that included herself and Karl.

Theoretically, Martha, Karl, and Helen were all
possible suspects in the sense that they either did

know or could have known of the appointment, but none of them could have done it themselves. They all had airtight alibis. Martha was being kidnapped and both Helen and Karl were highly visible at the time—Helen at Great Western and Karl at the Crescent Company. Which didn't leave me much in the way of suspects.

"And if that's the best I can do, Sam is right," I muttered. "I'm not qualified to investigate a homicide."

Of course, any one of them could have hired the killer. Or one of the four people (I included Peter Johnson) could have mentioned the appointment to a fifth party. A person who for some reason felt threatened by the idea of Johnson talking to a PI. That second someone could have either set up the hit, or done it himself.

It could have been a woman, of course, but I like the generic *he*. It's easier.

If Peter Johnson had talked to the wrong person it was going to be hard to track down but I was sure Helen would be able to remember whom, if anyone, she had told. Which left Karl.

Karl was a question mark in several ways. He not only could have talked to the wrong person, he was my choice for the one most likely to have hired the hit. His absentminded professor routine was too facile.

I could think of several motives for him, but at the moment they were pure guesswork. Almost anything was possible, and he did have what passed for opportunity. Also his coming to see me in the hospital had been odd and his parting comment to me this afternoon could actually have been a threat.

Yes, I would definitely have to check on Karl.

That left me with Martha's kidnapping, and Deke Long's death. I was sure they were connected—coincidence simply would not stretch to cover the three crimes—but again there was no tie-in between them. Deke Long and Peter Johnson were connected through Great Western but it was a tenuous thread at best and there was not a shred of connection between either of them and Martha.

I had covered six sheets of paper with scribbled notes, and it was getting light outside before I finally went back to sleep, but I wasn't much further ahead in my thinking. I had a lot of ideas but the big stumbling block was still there.

How had the rifleman known Peter Johnson was going to be in my office that afternoon?

THE TELEPHONE woke me at nine the next morning. It was Cass, full of morning cheer.

"Do you have a picnic basket?" he asked. "The kind you see on TV that holds dishes and knives and forks?"

He sounded so enthusiastic I had to laugh. "Believe it or not, I do have," I told him. "I won it in a raffle and it's very elegant. It even has a place for stemmed wineglasses."

"Great. Let's fill it up and have a picnic. I got a city map from the desk clerk last night and I found a dozen picnic spots on it. There's one place out by your house called Gas Works Park. The clerk told me it's right on a lake. Lake Union. We can watch the boats go by."

I was tempted.

"Oh, come on," he said as I hesitated. "I'm going home tomorrow. You'll never get a better offer."

"You are?" I asked, surprised. "I thought you said you were going to stay up here for a few days."

"I did mean to, but the old man wants me back. My boss, Sheriff Tate. So, how about it? Shall we have a picnic?"

I knew I ought to spend the day working but I told him I'd be ready by eleven o'clock.

"I'll be there," he said. "And in the meantime,

take your phone off the hook. I don't want you getting that better offer."

I hung up laughing, but I did switch the phone onto the answering machine. A picnic sounded like fun and I didn't want anything to interfere.

Cass arrived with a huge sack of deli food, two bottles of sparkling cider, and a mammoth fresh pineapple we had to slice before we could get it in the basket.

Despite it being a gorgeous Saturday we almost had the park to ourselves. There was a handful of teenagers down by the water and a couple of family groups up by the tanks. The west side was deserted. We spent the day there stretched out on a blanket in the sun, talking, watching the pleasure boats, finding out about each other.

His physical attraction was so strong it made my skin tingle—and I'm pretty sure it was mutual—but he didn't try to come on to me and I didn't make any overtures either. I don't know why. Maybe for once I was just using some common sense. I've had my share of romances that didn't work out. I'm not looking for a long-term relationship—the very idea of marriage turns me off—but neither am I one of the "your place or mine" group. Any kind of a relationship with Cass was bound to be a dead end. For one thing we lived half a continent apart. More important, however, despite his being warm and funny and sexy, he had some very hard edges. He had all the polish of a brick, and although I hate to generalize, he was what I think of as a typical macho Texan. Not even aware of being a chauvinist. I don't need that kind of aggravation.

Leaving, late in the afternoon, Cass took a wrong turn out of the parking lot and we ended up over by the University of Washington.

"Is it okay to drive through the campus?" he asked. "I started out in law enforcement working campus security at the University of Texas."

"Sure. It's Saturday, and I don't think school is on now anyway," I said. "We can circle around and stop at the Canoe House for a drink. The bar is on top of the building and it has a great view of Lake Washington."

"How many lakes are there in this town?" Cass asked. "That map I looked at last night had blue splashed all over it."

I named some of our more interesting waterways for him as we drove around the campus: Lake Washington, with two floating bridges, which stretched for miles along the eastern side of the city; Puget Sound, waterway to the Pacific, on the western side; with Lake Union, Green Lake, the ship canal, the Ballard locks, and innumerable small lakes all within the city limits. Coming from the high plains country, the idea of having that much water around fascinated him. Before we got to the Canoe House we had decided he needed to stay at least one more day so he could take a ferry ride.

We were laughing, making up silly excuses for him to give his boss, when we got off the elevator and went into the bar.

It was bright inside, the sun still pouring in through the windows, and the first person I saw was Sam Morgan. He was at the bar having a solitary drink. I wanted to turn around and leave, quick, before he saw us, but I didn't have the chance. Cass saw him at the same time I did and immediately steered me over there.

I had a feeling Sam was going to ruin the rest of my day.

He looked at us in the mirror and gave a perfunctory nod.

"You don't look too happy," Cass told him, signaling the bartender and pulling a stool around for me. "What's been sourin' your day?"

He ordered coffee for us both.

"Well?" he asked Sam. "Has something happened we don't know about?"

Sam shrugged. "Karl Johnson is dead."

"What?" I gaped at him. I had almost convinced myself that Karl was responsible for his father's death. How could he be dead?

"What happened?" Cass asked more sensibly.

"At the moment we aren't sure," Sam said wearily. "His mother, Barbara Johnson, found him floating in his bathtub at ten-thirty-five this morning."

"I thought she was in Rome," I said.

"She was. She arrived at Seatac at nine-fifteen this morning and when Karl didn't meet her plane like he was supposed to she took a cab to his apartment. She let herself in with her own key, and found him. I've been over there all afternoon. I just came from there now."

Cass frowned. "Why? It sounds like an accident. He was probably getting ready to go get her."

Sam gave him an odd look. "What makes you say that?"

"Well, it…I don't know. If he just got up and was hurrying, getting ready to go get his mother, and was maybe still half asleep? Easy to slip and fall."

Sam nodded. "Maybe. Except for one thing. His mother said he never took baths."

"Never took a bath?" Cass frowned.

"What...oh, just showers, you mean. But how does she know? I mean, if he has his own apartment she may not know as much about him as she thinks she does."

"She says he always took showers, never a bath, from the time he was a kid." Sam hesitated, waiting for Cass to comment, before going on. "His girlfriend says the same thing. As it happened she showed up a few minutes after I got there. Didn't know anything was wrong, of course. She's a Canadian. Only comes down on weekends."

"How nice for her," I said sourly, thinking of what a horrible shock she must have had.

"There was one other thing," Sam said slowly.

"Oh? What?" Cass asked.

"He couldn't have been hurrying to get his mother. He died late last night. And the M. E. doesn't think he fell either. Someone went to a lot of trouble to make it look like an accident, but there's a bruise on his forehead that's in the wrong place."

TEN

I WAS RIGHT ABOUT one thing. Sam did ruin the rest of my day.

Once he got started he told us all he knew about Karl's death, which suited Cass fine, but not me. I didn't want to hear about it, at least not right then.

His death was a shock, and it seemed to hit Cass hard. He kept coming back to the accident theory, picking at Sam for details, trying to make the facts fit into the mishap pattern he was sure was there.

Sam let him talk, saying he was too tired to argue with him. The case wasn't officially a homicide, and wouldn't be until the coroner gave him the word, but despite the lack of evidence we all knew Karl's death hadn't been an accident.

Although, as Sam said, the killer had almost committed the perfect crime. The only evidence, other than Barbara Johnson's word that Karl didn't ever take baths, was so iffy it could very easily have gone unnoticed.

Barbara had found Karl floating face down in the tub, but the massive bruise that seemed to be the cause of his drowning was on the back of his head. The coroner said the body could have turned as it cooled, or he could have turned as he fell. Either of which might have happened, but neither theory accounted for the smaller bruise on his forehead, nor the indentation in the center of it that matched the conical knob of the shower control above the tub faucet. Karl's body had been found facing away from the control, and there was no way it could have floated end for end in the cramped space of the tub. Not on its own.

Cass argued against murder as long as possible. As he said, no one had any reason to kill Karl, or at least no one that any of us knew of, but he couldn't explain the bruise on Karl's forehead either.

He finally gave up and took me home, letting me out in front of the house with an absentminded "good night," and no kiss.

It was still early, a few minutes after eight, so I decided I might as well get some work done. Peter Johnson's murder, and now Karl's, were the foremost things on my mind but I wasn't getting paid to investigate their deaths and I needed to catch up on some of the paying cases I was supposed to be working on.

I switched on the computer and transferred my notes from the night before to the Johnson file, then went to work organizing a report on a missing wife I'd located. The report took me well over an hour to complete. It was a little tricky. I'd found the woman easily enough. She had been born in Denver, so the first thing I checked was the new power hookups in the towns around the mile-high city, and there she was under her maiden name, but I wasn't sure I wanted to give her husband the information. At least not until I had done some more checking on the two emergency hospital reports I'd stumbled on.

I try never to cash a retainer until I'm sure I want the writer for a client. It's a lot easier to back out of a case if you have the original check. I still had this client's check in the safe. I had been dubious about taking his money to start with, but it was just a feeling, nothing concrete, and you can't run a business on that kind of feelings. So I had agreed to look for the woman. Now I was beginning to suspect the man was a wife-beater, and if so, I wasn't going to tell him where to find her. The problem was, I wasn't sure, and until I was sure I didn't want to antagonize him, hence my difficulty with the report. I wanted him to know I was making progress; I just didn't want to tell him anything.

I finally got the thing to sound the way I wanted

it and printed it out along with an employee background statement for a bonding company I'd finished before I left that morning. I also spent a few minutes organizing my notes for a report on Venetian shipping in the early eighteen-hundreds I was doing for one of my writer clients. I'd write it up on Monday.

My head was aching again and I was suddenly very tired. I didn't want to think about the Johnson case, nor even Cass Feliciano.

So I went upstairs and got ready for bed, perversely putting on a sheer chiffon nightgown that is too thin for the Seattle climate. I like the way it makes me feel. Glamorous. It's a pale peach color with satin trim in a soft coral shade, a gorgeous gown, but it isn't warm. I had to sit up in the middle of the night and pull my down comforter up over me.

Sunday, I was off work and off the human race. I spent the whole day lying around, pigging out on junk food and reading that new Ludlum book.

I did call Denver. Helen had given me the number. I wanted to talk to Dave Porter, the night watchman, about his seeing Johnson on Sunday night, but he was out fishing with his son-in-law. His daughter took my name and number and promised to have him call me when he came in. She said they would probably be late but I didn't care what time it was.

He called back finally a few minutes after eight that evening. He had heard about Peter Johnson's death from Sam and was a little hesitant about talking to me at first, but he loosened up some as we went along, especially after I told him Karl had been killed too.

I had already heard most of what he told me from Helen but he did add one thing that might have had some bearing on both murders. He said that Monday morning when he went off shift Karl had been in the warehouse office talking to two of the drivers and that he, Dave, had stopped to chat with them. He also told them about Peter Johnson having been in the warehouse all night. Which meant that any number of people, including the killer, could have known that he'd been searching for something.

I also finally heard from my juvenile snitch, Joey Winters. He and his parents had been out of town on vacation for a week. When he got home a friend had given him the word I was looking for him so, as he said, he hustled on over to see me, arriving shortly after I finished talking to Dave. Joey was properly horrified that I'd been shot—he seems to think he's responsible for me—and promised to get cracking on the case first thing in the morning. His words, not mine.

I thought he'd be more successful than the law when it came to the neighborhood. The police hadn't been able to turn up a single witness and they had been doing a door-to-door, but they didn't have Joey's resources. In addition to being an inveterate busybody, Joey knew every kid for blocks around. One of them might have seen or heard something, and in the natural order of things they might not tell an adult. They would tell Joey.

MONDAY MORNING was beautiful. Sunny and warm, with blue skies and fleecy white clouds. I showered, fluffed up my wig, put on my new Liz Claiborne outfit, and was ready to go. I never eat breakfast at home on a workday. I do usually stop at the little French patisserie near the office and pick up a couple of fresh croissants and coffee, but I didn't bother this morning.

I wanted to sort out the information I had on Karl's death before I forgot anything, but mainly I wanted to talk to Sam before he got too busy. I was hoping he would let me see the report from the Texas authorities on the death of the two young men there. He'd told me he'd called them Friday morning and asked to have it faxed to him.

I got to the office a few minutes after eight and found Martha standing in the middle of the reception room when I opened the door. She looked both angry and fearful.

"What's wrong?" I nearly yelled at her, frightened by her expression. I'm definitely not heroic.

"Nothing. Don't yell at me."

"I'm sorry. But what's wrong?"

"Nothing's wrong. You startled me. I just came in. It's the first time I've been in here since those…" She stopped for a second, scowling. "I remembered how scared I was and it made me mad. I'd like to get those lowlifes, I would."

"You make a stunning Valkyrie, Martha," I told her. "But don't get carried away. From what I hear, if you're talking about the New Janizary gang, they hurt people."

She nodded, scowling. "They do that. They have the whole area around the south end of the lake terrorized. There was another drive-by shooting down there last week that was attributed to them."

"How do you know?"

"I went down there yesterday and talked—"

"You what?" I gasped, interrupting her. "Are you crazy? You know what that part of town is like. And don't think you're safe just because you're black. If they caught you snooping into their business those toughs wouldn't give a hoot what color you were. Did you go down there alone?''

"Of course not. Charles went with me.''

"Oh, no! You *are* crazy. Black you and white Charles? What happened?''

Martha glared at me for a moment, then started to laugh. "For heaven's sake, Demary,'' she said between chuckles. "I'm not an idiot. And neither is Charles. I know he acts like he has feathers for brains but he's quite sharp in his way. Neither of us are silly enough to accost someone on the street and ask them what they think of the New Janizary gang, you know.''

"Well, what did you do?''

"We went to see Mr. Percy. You remember him? You did an employee check for him last year. He has that big appliance store down there.''

"Oh, yes. I remember him,'' I said, relieved. "What did he tell you? Does he know any of the Janizary gang?''

"No, of course not. He doesn't know anything about them except what he's read in the papers, but he does hear all the local gossip and he told us one really interesting story. He said there's a rumor the gang has police protection.''

"Police protection? That's crazy. One of their

crack houses was raided just a couple of weeks ago, and I think two of the gang were busted. What kind of protection is that? I don't believe it.''

Martha shrugged. ''Actually, I don't either, but I do think they may have an informant.''

''What do you mean?''

''After talking with Mr. Percy I checked with a gal I know at the newspaper, and one thing kind of stands out if you know what you're looking for. The gang always seems to be one step ahead of the law. It's almost as if they were being tipped off on time, place, and so forth. And if there is a bad cop keeping them informed of what's going down, that could be what started the protection story.''

''Mmm, yes. That could be so,'' I said, turning the idea over in my mind. I didn't question what she said—if Martha said there was a pattern, there was—but I couldn't see where it got us. There was still no reason I could think of for the Janizary gang to have kidnapped her to start with. And given their reputation, no reason for them letting her go so tamely once they had her. Nor could I see any connection between them and Johnson.

We talked it over for a while, but we couldn't come up with anything new. Martha said she had been thinking about what she'd heard the men say, trying to think of anything that would give us a lead, but nothing she remembered seemed to have any significance. What few words she'd heard all had to do with driving or where they were going, without giving any clue as to where they had started from or what their purpose was.

My phone rang at nine-thirty, breaking up a futile discussion we were having about motives.

It was Sam. Karl's death was officially murder.

ELEVEN

SAM SAID I COULD see the report they had sent him from Texas, provided I did my looking in his office. He wouldn't give me a copy. I didn't argue. I was surprised he'd let me see it at all after the fight we'd had at McRory's.

I told him I'd be right down, grabbed my purse, and was on my way out when the phone rang again. Martha took the call and waved me back into my office.

It was the widow, Barbara Johnson. She listened politely to my words of condolence, then cut to the reason for her call.

"Miss Jones, I'd like to see you as soon as possible," she said briskly. "I need to talk to you, but I have a rather tight schedule this morning. Would you be willing to come out here to the Great Western offices, rather than my coming to your office?"

"Well, yes, I think I can do that," I said. I couldn't guess from her tone what she had in mind but I wanted to see her anyway, so whatever she wanted was okay with me. I did start to say something else but before I could get the words out she spoke again.

"Would right now be a satisfactory time?"

I said it would be fine and she hung up.

"She sounds like her husband," Martha, who had listened in, said.

"Too much like him," I agreed, annoyed by the woman's abrupt manner. "I wonder if she knows why he really wanted that telephone tap."

"One way to find out."

I nodded. "I'll ask, all right, but if she's as much like him as she sounds I won't find out from her. Although maybe she wants to hire me for the same thing. Seems strange that she would be at work so soon after Karl's death."

"She may not actually be working. For Great Western, I mean. She may just be using the office to take care of... You know, the funerals, all that."

"I guess."

MRS. JOHNSON MET ME in the doorway of her husband's office, shook hands, and waved me to the same rickety plastic chair. She didn't apologize for the chair, nor for the office, which was as shabby as ever. She didn't strike me as the type who apologized for anything, nor did she show any sign of her terrible double loss. She seemed quite calm and self-possessed. Which didn't mean much, of course. Everyone handles grief in their own way.

She was a tall woman with light-brown hair pulled back into a smooth bun, brown eyes, and high cheekbones. She had a beautiful figure. Her suit, an expensive-looking royal-blue silk creation, fit her to perfection. With it she wore a cream-colored blouse and navy scarf.

She got right down to business. "I asked Helen Wagoner about you," she said. "She told me what she knew, or had been told about you, plus, of course, Peter must have thought you were competent or he wouldn't have gone to you to start with." She gave me a faint smile. "You probably wish he hadn't. However, be that as it may, you're involved whether you like it or not. And you are a private investigator. So, I'd like to hire you."

"To do what, Mrs. Johnson?"

She gave me a rather surprised look. "To proceed with whatever Peter wanted, and to find out who killed him, and my son, of course. What did you think I meant? And please call me Barbara. I'm not as formal as Peter was and hearing 'Mrs. Johnson' always makes me look for my mother-in-law."

"All right, Barbara, if you'll call me Demary. And I didn't expect anything in particular. But the thing is, I'm not a private investigator. Not the kind I think you want, nor what your husband wanted. I explained that to him.''

A slight frown creased her forehead. "I don't understand. What do you mean?"

I explained what I did, then went on. "I don't know why your husband came to see me either, and I was hoping you would know. I thought you might want the same thing.''

She shook her head. "I have no idea what Peter wanted. I've been gone for six weeks and, from what Helen has told me, whatever was bothering him happened after I left. I think you'll have to find out what it was, though, because it's probably the reason for his death. And I'd still like to hire you.''

I thought a minute. She watched me with steady eyes.

"I'll find out what I can about their deaths," I said finally. "Whoever shot your husband came within a fraction of an inch of killing me too, so I have a lively interest in finding him. Or her. But, to be honest, this really isn't my line of work. I'm not one of those private-eye characters like on TV. I do some skip-tracing and missing persons, but mostly I research and collect facts and figures for insurance companies, lawyers, and writers." I stopped, thought a moment, then went on.

"Most of the information I collect is in the public domain and most of my sources—libraries, newspapers, government records—are available to anyone with the time and skill to use them. Some, such as city, state, and federal records, take time and patience to unravel but the information is there for anyone who knows where to look and has the ability to run a computer. I've never investigated a murder before, and truthfully, I'd be an unnecessary expense for you. I don't have the resources the police department has, and Lieutenant Morgan is—"

"I've met Lieutenant Morgan," she interrupted, "and while I don't doubt his capabilities I also know how the police department works. Finding my son's murderer will be only one of several cases he'll be working on. You can, if you wish, devote your entire time to finding him. Or her. And as far as expense, or resources, are concerned, I am a very wealthy woman and I am quite willing to spend whatever is necessary."

I liked the sound of that. "All right," I said, making up my mind. I was going to work on it anyway so I might as well get paid for my efforts. "I'll see what I can do."

"How much retainer do you want?"

"A thousand will do to start with. I charge forty dollars an hour plus expenses. I'll give you an itemized bill and a refund if it's called for."

She didn't even hesitate. She took a checkbook out of the desk drawer and started writing. She was certainly a woman of few words.

"Anything else?" she asked, handing the check across to me.

"Yes. I'd like to have my secretary come to work here in the office, but I don't want anyone to know she works for me. Except Helen Wagoner."

"Why? What do you want her to do?"

"I want her to search the computer files to see if she can trace what your husband was working on Monday morning when Helen Wagoner came to work. I don't know that it will have anything to do with his murder but we need to be sure."

"Very well, I'll tell personnel to put her on as a computer operator."

"If you don't mind I'd rather she came in as your personal secretary. It would give her more freedom to move around."

"All right. I'll see to it. Is there anything I should know about her? Am I supposed to know her already?"

"Mmm, yes. You can say she has worked for you before. She's black, beautiful, comes from

Barbados, and is an expert computer operator. That's probably all you need to know. She'll come in as an employee, not as a friend.''

Barbara Johnson nodded and stood up. "If you want anything else later just tell Helen," she said. "But if you learn anything, anything at all, about whoever was responsible, call me. I know my husband struck most people as overbearing, possibly unpleasant, but that was no reason to kill him. I cared about him and about my son. I don't want a lot of written reports, but I want to be kept up-to-date on the progress of your investigation. Agreed?''

I told her I agreed, shook hands, and left. Thinking about her as I went looking for Helen Wagoner, I found that I liked Barbara Johnson despite her cool manner. Which surprised me. I hadn't expected to.

Helen was waiting for me in the reception room. She took me back to her office and we settled the details of Martha's coming to work the next morning.

"She's going to be looking for whatever it was Peter Johnson was putting on the computer," I told Helen. "I don't think she will need any help, other than maybe a starting point, but you will have to decide how she can best be introduced to the rest

of the people around here. If there is even an outside chance that the murderer is in the office, or
has an informant in the office, I don't want anyone
wondering about her.''

''Hmm, yes, I see that. Just bringing her in as
Mrs. Johnson's secretary won't do. No one will
expect her to be doing any regular work but she
will need some reason for accessing computer records. How about if I say she has been employed
by Mrs. Johnson's accountant? She can be looking
for figures relating to the inheritance taxes Barbara
will have to pay because Karl and Mr. J. died
within thirty days of each other.''

''Oh? Will she have to pay extra taxes?'' I
asked. I didn't remember anything like that from
when I was doing bookkeeping. However, Con-
gress changes the tax laws more often than they
do their shirts, so I could believe it easily enough.

''I don't have any idea,'' she said with a shrug.
''It sounds convincing, though.''

I laughed. ''All right, that should do it then.
She'll be here tomorrow morning. Now, I'd like to
ask you a few questions about Karl.''

Without any warning at all Helen's professional
facade crumpled into a mask of tears. I was so
surprised I sat there like a lump while she buried
her face in her hands and cried. I had no idea she

thought that much of Karl, although I did remember Peter Johnson's obvious lie about an affair between Karl and Helen being the reason for the wiretap. I didn't even know what to say, although I did try to console her with a few well-meant, if inane, words of sympathy.

"I'll be all right," she said finally, mopping her face with a tissue. "Stupid of me. I can't imagine why I broke down like that. I was fond of Karl; he was a very nice person." She gave me a fierce look. "I know he struck most people as inept, but he wasn't. He was just terribly shy."

"Shy?"

I must have sounded doubtful because she came back at me with a snap. "Yes, shy. He certainly wasn't the bungling Mr. Malaprop you probably thought he was. In fact, he was brilliant in some respects. He was the one who set up our computer system, and he also organized the truck routing. The routing saved the company thousands of dollars and he did that while he was still in college." She wiped her eyes again and smiled a suddenly hard smile. "I know it sounds silly, but I'd really like to have a few minutes alone with whoever killed him."

"You'd probably get yourself killed," I said irritably. People who say that kind of thing are idiots. Murderers are, by definition, murderous. The law-abiding are seldom any match for such people, and a fragile woman like Helen Wagoner certainly wouldn't be.

"I don't care," she said, blowing her nose. "What did you want to ask me about Karl?"

"To start with, do you know if he was in his father's office Monday? After ten in the morning?"

"Monday?" She rubbed her forehead. "I-I'm not sure."

"Think. That was the day it all started. You took Dave, the night watchman, to the airport and when you got to the office Peter Johnson was working on the computer in your office. Do you remember that day?"

"Yes, of course I do, but I can't specifically remember Karl going into...wait...let me think. Yes, that was the day they were talking about changing the routings in northern New Mexico. He was with his father for almost an hour. Why? I mean, if I know what you're looking for maybe I can help."

I explained my problem with Peter Johnson's appointment.

"Someone had to know about it in advance in order for the gunman to be there at the right time,"

I said. "With Karl's death we now know for sure that it wasn't a random shooting. Someone specifically wanted Peter Johnson dead. On Monday morning only he and Martha knew about the appointment. Martha didn't mention it to anyone and she keeps her appointment book in a locked drawer, so the information didn't come from my office. It had to come from here. Now, you've already told me you didn't see the notation on his desk calendar until Tuesday morning, but did you mention it to anyone after that? Could Karl have seen it on Monday or Tuesday morning? Could anyone else have seen it at any time? And last, do you think Peter Johnson himself would, or did, tell anyone he was going to see me?"

She sat, frowning at me, thinking, for several minutes. "To start with, no, I don't think Mr. Johnson would have told anyone, and I certainly didn't say anything to anyone about it. Karl could have seen it, of course; I have no way of knowing. He didn't say anything. What I was trying to remember was if anyone else was in his office that morning. I don't think there was. He had no appointments. I've already checked. I suppose someone could have gotten into the office Monday night but it doesn't seem very likely."

"No, probably not. But speaking of appointments, how about Karl's appointment book? Have you checked it? Who did he see on Monday and Tuesday?''

''No one in a business way, not here anyway. Neither one of them kept me informed about their appointments, though. I didn't know a thing about that Texas policeman until he got here. Karl had a dinner engagement with someone on Monday, but that was in the evening.''

''Who? And how do you know about his evening engagements?''

''I don't know who,'' she said slowly. ''But I know about that date because whoever it was with called here around noon on Monday. He has called before and I should remember his name, but I...'' Her voice trailed off; in a minute she made a face and went on. ''No, I can't think of the name but maybe it will come to me later. At any rate, whoever it was, he called that morning while I was in Karl's office and as he hung up Karl said he was going out to dinner—''

We were interrupted by a svelte-looking brunet with huge blue eyes and the vocal delivery of a riveting gun. She stuck her head in the door and told Helen something that didn't seem to please either of them. She talked so fast I didn't understand a word she said.

"I'm sorry, I've got to go," Helen said briskly, already halfway out the door. "Call me this afternoon if you want anything else."

She was gone before I could reply.

TWELVE

I TOOK THE OLD Interurban Avenue back into downtown Seattle. I needed to think and I didn't feel like bucking the traffic on Interstate 5. Bits and pieces were beginning to stick together in my mind but I still couldn't come up with any kind of a motive for the killings. And without a motive, trying to find the murderer looked pretty hopeless. The field was too open.

None of the obvious motives fit. Gain was usually on top of the list, but it didn't seem to fit here.

My gut feeling was that Peter Johnson had been killed to keep him from talking about something. It was probably something to do with the company, and very likely to do with the warehouse. The motive for Karl's murder might be the same, but he could also have learned something about his father's death that endangered the killer.

I agreed with Barbara Johnson that the motive almost had to be something connected with her husband wanting to hire me, but if so, why hadn't the killer shot him as he went into the office instead of waiting until he came out? And why hadn't he taken a crack at me again? The only possible answer to the second half of that question had to be that he knew Peter Johnson had not told me anything. Which meant he was either someone I knew, or he was close enough to someone I'd confided in to be getting information from them without their knowing it. A very spooky idea.

Halfway to downtown Seattle I stopped in the little township of Tukwila and went into a grocery store for a can of cola and a sack of chips. Junk food isn't my normal fare but I was hungry and it didn't look as if I was going to have time to stop anywhere for a meal.

Tukwila is a neat place. It's an old-fashioned kind of farm town with a population of around 2,000. Totally surrounded by the greater metropolis of Seattle, it has resisted repeated annexation efforts, never surrendering its individuality. The roads are blacktop, and there aren't any sidewalks; the edges of the roads just kind of blend into the yards and truck gardens. Big old trees line the streets, arching out to form a green tunnel over your head as you drive along. Some of the houses go back to the Victorian era and there are still a few cows and horses in fenced pastures.

I was sorry to get back into the hustle and bustle of the city traffic.

Sam was in the main squad room when I got there. He took me into his office and handed over the Texas report without my even asking. He acted strange, and I didn't understand why he was being so cooperative, but I wasn't about to look a gift-horse in the mouth. I settled down to read it while he started filling in the blanks on some kind of a form.

The report didn't add anything to what Cass had already told us. It didn't mention Cass by name, referring to him throughout as "the officer in charge." You would think in a town the size of Valentine they could dispense with officialese, but I guess bureaucracies are the same everywhere.

It didn't mention the inquiries he had made in Albuquerque either, which did seem a little strange. I wondered if Cass had told us the truth about that. He may have gone up there on his own.

After I finished reading I put the file folder down on the desk and sat staring at the wall for a minute.

"Well? Did you get anything new out of it?" Sam asked.

"No, but to tell the truth I don't know what I'm looking for," I said honestly. "Something about it doesn't feel right, though."

"How so?"

I shook my head. I didn't know. "It's all there, every single thing Cass told us, but it doesn't read right somehow. It reads more like a movie script. It sounds like, uh, like a western cowboy show."

Sam sighed. "It *is* western. That's where I got it. From a Texas sheriff. And yes, the wording is a little different than we use here on the coast, but believe me, Texas lawmen aren't any kind of hick cops. I've dealt with a few Texans before."

"I guess you're right, but..." I shrugged. There was still something odd about the report but I couldn't put my finger on what it was, so there was no use worrying about it. Maybe it would come to me later.

We talked for a while and I told him about Barbara Johnson hiring me. I expected him to be furious, but he didn't say anything at all. I left a few minutes later.

Joey called me that evening a few minutes before eight o'clock. "I haven't found any grade-A eyeballs," he informed me. "I got a line on a better witness, though, and I wanted to tell you the cops are working the wrong side of the block."

"What do you mean, the wrong side of the block?" I asked, when I'd figured out what he said.

I don't know where Joey gets his slang. Sometimes he sounds like he's from another planet.

"They're asking questions on Forty-fifth. If the perp had any smarts he came up the back way, through the courtyard behind the Alhambra."

"The what?"

"The Alhambra. That's the name of the apartment."

"It is?"

"It's carved over the door," Joey said patiently. "Anyway, that must have been how he got in."

"How? What are you talking about? The courtyard doesn't have an outside entrance. It's like an air shaft; it's surrounded by other buildings."

Joey's exasperated sigh was a little overdone. He can be a real wise guy.

"Those other buildings have windows that look out on the same courtyard, and some of the buildings have entrances on Forty-sixth Street, and they have basements, and the basements have more windows, and you can climb out those windows into the courtyard."

"Darn. So that's why no one saw him."

"Right."

I told him he was doing a great job, which was what he wanted to hear, and was about to hang up when I remembered what he'd said to start with. He'd said he had a line on a ''better'' witness.

''Well, all I got so far is Bobbie Crenshaw, Tommy Crenshaw's brother,'' Joey explained. ''He saw some woman in the courtyard but that was after the cop, so I don't think she counts.''

I thought a minute. ''No, I guess not. What time did he see her?''

''Well, that's kinda the problem. He can't tell time yet. He's only five. He just knows he saw her after he saw the cop. But don't worry, I got another possibility cooking. I'll turn up something.''

I barely managed to hang up before I collapsed on the couch whooping with laughter. I had some sharp investigators working for me, all right. A mouthy teenager and a five-year-old. I was glad I'd never told anyone about Joey.

Sometime in the middle of the night I woke up thinking about Cass. While I'm not the proverbial ice maiden, I don't take up with just anyone either. I'm picky. The guy and the timing have to be right. And despite my original thinking about Texans, I had come to the conclusion that it was right with Cass. If it hadn't been for meeting Sam at the Canoe House—and his telling us about Karl—Cass and I might have ended the evening differently.

But now, out of the blue, I decided I didn't want to see him again. I didn't brood about it; I went right back to sleep, but the decision was still with me when I woke up. It was based on an ambivalent impression that wasn't strong enough to put a label on but was too solid to ignore. The thought left me feeling dull and gloomy all day.

THIRTEEN

TUESDAY WAS A REAL BLANK for me. Martha went to work at Great Western that morning but I didn't make any progress on anything. It's like that sometimes. You hit a dry spell when nothing seems to jell.

I didn't hear from Cass either, which surprised me a little. I knew he hadn't left town because I talked to Sam Tuesday afternoon and he said he'd seen Cass earlier in the day.

I still had that indefinable uneasy feeling whenever I thought of Cass so I was glad he didn't call, but I wished I could figure out what was bothering me. I didn't like him any less; I just had this funny feeling.

I spent a lot of time on the computer balancing one fact against another, sifting information on the killings. Sometimes it helps to see things on the screen instead of in your head. Not this time, though. Even without a motive I could make a case against several of the people involved but I still came up against the same old stumbling blocks.

I was at my desk in the office when Martha called Wednesday afternoon.

"I found it," she said, a thread of excitement running through her voice. "The whole story. It was in the inventory files under coke. Right between chocolate and cherry syrup. Coke for cocaine."

"Of course!" I said, recognizing the connection. "He told me. Or tried to. That's what he cried out as he fell, just before the last shot hit him. It sounded like he said, 'Luck is a ventry fly.' But he was saying 'look.' Not luck, look. Look. Look in the inventory files. Well, what did you find? Or what did *he* find?"

"He found about twenty-five pounds of pure Colombian cocaine. The weight is a guess but he was pretty exact about the rest of it."

"No wonder he got shot. Does he say—"

"I'm printing it out now," Martha interrupted. "I just wanted to make sure you were in the office. I'll be there in about forty-five minutes."

It wasn't a very well-written document; parts of it were repetitious and confusing, but it held some explosive information. Condensed, what Peter Johnson said was this:

On Monday, June 11, in Albuquerque, he learned that a Texas lawman had been snooping around the Great Western warehouse, asking the drivers questions about a murder. He called Sheriff Tate in Valentine to find out what was going on and was told about the two dead young men.

When he got back to Seattle he began investigating on his own, starting with the truck mileage records. He worked at night and, as he wasn't familiar with the computer, it took him nearly two weeks to match up all the records. Once he figured out how to work the machine, however, he found what he was looking for.

The trucks on the El Paso/Fort Stanton/Roswell/Albuquerque run were driving seventy to one hundred miles more than normal every third or fourth trip. And those trips coincided with the arrival or departure from Albuquerque of one of the company's eighteen-wheelers that moved selected merchandise to and from the central warehouses.

From there he went to sales and invoices. Again it took him a while, but he finally spotted the kind of thing he was sure would be there.

When starting out, all the route trucks were loaded with standard items, to which the drivers added items that had been ordered by specific customers, or items they thought would sell well in their territory. The truck inventory was checked as it was loaded and again when the truck returned, and as long as invoices and inventory matched, the driver's choices weren't questioned, or apparently even noticed.

The records showed that on every long-mileage trip the trucks in question carried several extra cases of a slow-moving item such as individual hot chocolate packets in July, or iced tea in December. Cases that were never sold and were eventually returned to the warehouse.

In Peter Johnson's words:

As soon as I spotted that fact I knew what the mechanics were. The driver of the route truck picks up the cocaine at some prearranged spot in south Texas, places it in a case of whatever merchandise is decided upon beforehand, meets the eighteen-wheeler somewhere near Albuquerque, and exchanges the cartons containing cocaine for the same number of cartons containing regular merchandise. The cocaine is carried on to its destination, which is probably Seattle. All inventories remain correct so no questions arise.

The two side trips, to pick up the cocaine and to exchange cases with the eighteen-wheeler, accounted for the extra mileage.

Peter Johnson then started to search the Seattle warehouse for some clue as to how the cocaine cases were marked. He found it on Sunday night. An easy-to-spot and simple triple X in bright-blue marker pencil on the side of two cases of individual hot chocolate packets. Bright blue being the usual color of the legitimate printing on the box, it wasn't obvious, and, if it was noticed, it would probably be thought to be a factory mark.

That left him with the last and most important factor as far as he was concerned. Who was the man, or men, behind the scheme?

At that point the file ended.

"So he came to me for a phone tap," I said, tossing the printout onto my desk. "Why the heck didn't he tell me the truth? If I'd known what it was all about I'd have set him up with Brownlee. He does taps all the time."

"Because he was afraid. Afraid Karl was in on the scheme. I think that's why he kept his suspicions to himself and why he tried to find the cocaine cartons himself. Why he didn't hire anyone until he felt he had to," Martha said, frowning at her reflection in the mirrored wall behind my desk. She got up and paced back and forth across the room, straightening a chair, tweaking dead leaves off a plant hanging in the corner.

"Karl had a lot more to do with running the company than it must have appeared from the way you described him," she said slowly. "And one of his main responsibilities was inventory control. He was in an ideal position to set up and work this kind of a deal."

"Do you think he did?"

Martha thought for a moment, then shook her head. "No, I don't."

"Any special reason?"

"Several reasons, and personally I can't understand why Peter J. didn't see the same things I saw. But I suppose when it concerns your only child you don't think all that clearly. Number one, according to everyone I talked to, without exception, Karl was very fond of his father, and he was wealthy in his own right so he didn't need money. If the office gossip is even close to the truth he not only wouldn't have done anything to hurt the old man, he would have done anything he possibly could to prevent his being hurt. And second, this scheme is pretty sharp, all right, but it does have a couple of big holes in it. From what I've heard about him I think Karl was too smart to be mixed up in anything that chancy."

"What holes?" I asked. I couldn't see anything that big.

"The biggest hole is the one they fell into. One or both of those boys in Texas found the stuff accidentally. In order for the thing to work the cocaine had to be carried almost openly. A variation on the Poe story, 'The Purloined Letter.' The stuff was stashed in a carton that had to be left in an open truck whenever the driver was making a delivery. To have locked the doors every time he carried any supplies into a restaurant would have invited suspicion."

"And I suppose the other was the mileage."

"Right. Mileage and gas consumption. Personally, I'm surprised that wasn't spotted right away; it's pretty obvious once you know what to look for, but apparently no one ever questioned the drivers."

I lifted the edge of my wig and scratched my head, trying to think. My own hair was beginning to grow out and the stubble itched.

"So, we've got the motive. Now all we need to do is to figure out who's behind it. Have you had a chance to look at any of the personnel records, Martha?"

"A few, but I have to be a little careful accessing those particular files. Mrs. Johnson's inheritance taxes will only cover so much."

"You be careful. *Very* careful. Whoever it is has

killed two people already. He won't balk at a third, and we sure can't count on him—or them—letting you go like before."

"Don't worry," she said. "I'm not wanting to join the dearly departed. I programmed a single-key screen-clear into the computer I'm using so I can blank out whatever I'm looking at when anyone comes too close to my desk."

"Well, be sure," I warned her. "You might make another printout of this for Sam Morgan, though. I'll have to tell him what you've found."

"Forget Morgan," she said, making an inelegant gesture. "Let him find his own stuff."

I grinned. Martha and Sam weren't terribly fond of each other.

FOURTEEN

CASS WAS SITTING on my front steps when I got home a little after six that evening. He not only had on his cowboy boots and hat, he was wearing a leather vest and a bolo tie with a slide featuring a huge chunk of turquoise. He looked like a character out of a B-grade western, not the mysterious figure I'd been building up in my mind.

He greeted me with a bear hug and a bourbon-scented kiss. He wasn't really drunk, just mellow, and immensely pleased with himself for some reason.

"C'mon, sugar," he said in an exaggerated drawl. "Let's you and me go out and paint the town red."

"Sounds good to me," I assured him as I unlocked my door and hauled him inside. No sense in giving the neighbors a show. "Just let me change first."

I took him on into the front room, plopped him into a chair, and raced up to my bedroom. I didn't want him following me upstairs so I did a fast job of getting into an old pair of Wrangler jeans, shirt, and boots.

He had reservations at a place on Aurora Avenue. A very elegant place. At first I didn't think they were going to let us in because of the way we were dressed, but a good-sized tip and Cass's accent changed the headwaiter's mind.

From there we went to a fishermen's tavern in Ballard. We had a beer and Cass got everybody singing "Home on the Range." Eventually we ended up back at the Canoe House where we watched the lights on the water and talked. I wondered where he'd been for the last four days but I didn't ask. We didn't discuss the case, and I forgot to tell him about the file Martha had found.

Actually, from early in the evening until I told him to go home we were engaged in a sort of subliminal battle of wills that left me totally exhausted, dissatisfied, keyed up, and angry. In a sense I was fighting him off all evening without us ever touching, but mainly I was fighting myself. It would be so easy to fall in love with Cass. My heart was certainly all for the idea. My head didn't agree, and I have finally reached the age where my head usually has the last word.

It had been a long time since my better judgment and I had that kind of a clash.

Later—sometime around three, just before I finally fell asleep—I thought of Sam and wondered why, as much as I liked him, Sam didn't have that kind of romantic appeal. He had everything else, and I knew he could be both passionate and tender, but he didn't send sparks up my spine.

I checked in with Barbara Johnson the next morning and gave her a copy of the file Martha had found on the computer. She was coming out of the building just as I drove up so we only had a minute, but I didn't mind. My main reason for going out to Great Western was to see Helen Wagoner. A remark she'd made the first time I'd talked to her had been drifting around the edge of my mind ever since, and that morning while I was brushing my teeth I finally realized why it bothered me.

Helen had said Karl had told her Deke Long had spent some time talking to Sam. He'd mentioned it to her on Wednesday morning. Sam had talked to everyone in the warehouse. Why had Karl particularly noticed him talking to Deke Long?

Unless, and this was taking a big jump into speculation, Karl had his eye on Deke for some reason. Maybe because of the smuggling operation? Had his father confided in him after all?

I didn't have anything to support the idea, but it

was possible. And there had to be some reason for
Karl to mention a warehouseman by name, or to
even know his name. Great Western employed
twenty-four men in and around the two warehouses, not counting the drivers. Did Karl know
all of them by name?

Helen couldn't help me. She was positive about
what Karl had said, but she couldn't think of any
reason why he'd know Deke's name or why Karl
would have his eye on Deke.

She did have one small bit of new information
for me, though. She'd remembered something
about Karl's dinner date on Monday evening.

"He said the man he was having dinner with
was an old friend from school," Helen told me.

"Did he mention the guy's name?"

"No, I don't think so. So much has happened I
can't..." Helen stopped and rubbed her forehead.
"No, he didn't mention the name. He wasn't talking to me, anyway; he was talking to his father. I
just happened to overhear them. He said he was
going to the Fractured Goose for dinner, and when
his father asked him who with, he said a friend
from school."

"A second ago you said 'old friend.' Which was
it?"

"Just friend, I think. Does it make a difference?"

"Probably not," I said. "But old friend might mean someone he hadn't seen for a long time."

"No, I told you, didn't I? The man has called here before. I recognized the voice."

"Which could mean that he lives in Seattle," I said. "Did Karl go to school here?"

"I don't know where he went to school, except college, of course. He went to the University of Texas in El Paso."

"Find out from Barbara where he went to grade school, and high school, will you please? Ask her as soon as she gets back and let me know right away."

Helen nodded.

I went from Great Western back downtown to Sam's office. I had a copy of the computer printout for him and I wanted to see Deke Long's record. Sam wasn't there but he was expected back any minute, so I decided to wait for him. Deke Long was beginning to interest me a whole lot; I wanted to know more about him.

While I waited I filled in the time flirting with a new man, Jake Allenby, who had been transferred from Bellevue. After a while a woman officer I knew, Carol Ann Guginsberg, came in. Neither Jake nor Carol Ann were working the Johnson case but they did know all about Deke Long's death. Carol Ann told me the lab men had proved a pair of leather sandals found near the alley that night had been worn by Deke.

"How did they do that?" I asked.

"Body dander."

"Where did they find them? I mean, were they together, like he had taken them off meaning to put something else on?"

"No, one was at the end of the alley, and I think the other was about a half block away lying in the street."

"Hmm. I wonder why they were so far apart?"

"He may have been running, trying to getaway from his killer," Carol Ann said. "They were the slip-on kind. He could have run right out of them."

"Sounds logical."

"I don't know enough about the case to speculate, but it is possible. Especially so as I think I remember one of the guys saying there were blood spots on the street near the sandal they found out there. You knew they identified the murder weapon, didn't you?"

"No. Where? And when?"

"Well, actually, they found it that same night but they didn't know for sure until they got the lab report yesterday," Carol Ann said. "Morgan says it's a hunting knife. They found it at the end of the alley, not too far from the body. It had been wiped off but there was still a lot of blood on it. Enough to identify it as the murder weapon anyway."

I remembered the knife. Someone had handed it to Sam in a plastic bag.

"Prints?" I asked.

"No. It has some kind of a fancy ivory grip that doesn't take prints."

"Elkhorn," Jake corrected. "An elkhorn grip."

Carol Ann had some new information on Karl's death too. The waitress who served Karl his dinner Friday night had called and talked to Sam. She had been out of town for three days and had not heard about his murder until she got back.

"She said Karl came in a few minutes after seven that night, Friday, and left at eight-fifteen," Carol Ann said. "So the coroner was able to narrow down the time of his death to between eleven and one in the morning. And she also may have seen the perp."

"How, and where?"

"Karl left his credit card on the table. She knew where he lived so she put it in her pocket and was going to drop it through the slot in his mailbox. She said his apartment is only a couple of blocks from the restaurant and she goes past the place on her way home. When she got there, though, she changed her mind. It was dark—she gets off at ten-thirty—and she saw a man standing in the shadow of the building, so she didn't stop.''

"Smart girl.''

"Right. No matter who it was,'' Carol Ann agreed.

"Did she have any kind of a description?''

"No, not really. She said he was tall, and she thought he was wearing a hat.''

"A hat? What kind of a hat?''

"She didn't know. She only had a momentary glimpse of him. Her lights picked him out as she came around the corner, so she didn't even slow down.''

"Not much to go on.''

"No, but if it was the perp at least you can elim-inate female pygmies as suspects,'' she said, laugh-ing.

Carol Ann has a primitive sense of humor.

Sam showed up about then. He was pleased with the file, but he wasn't at all pleased about Martha snooping around Great Western and we ended up having another row. He wouldn't show me any of the crime-scene reports and he refused to let me see Deke Long's rap sheet too. He was so crabby I couldn't believe it.

I couldn't figure out what was the matter with him. The day before he had handed over the report from Texas as nice as anything; today he was acting as if Deke's record was a top-priority secret. I was so mad at him by the time I left I nearly broke the glass in his office door slamming it behind me on my way out.

FIFTEEN

THE ANSWERING MACHINE at the office had a message from Sergeant Jean Clausen. She wanted to see me and would come by my office at three-thirty.

It was ten after three then. She hadn't given me much notice. I checked the thing by remote at noon.

She arrived five minutes later. She seemed nervous and after asking me how I felt, and admiring my wig, she said, "Demary, I asked around about you and most of the people I talked to said you were good at keeping your mouth shut. Are you?"

I shrugged. "Depends on what I hear. And where I hear it. I mean, if you're about to tell me you cheat on your income taxes I'll probably keep it to myself, but if you're going to tell me you shot Peter Johnson, that's another story."

She didn't laugh. "No, nothing like..." She stopped and made a face. "I made up my mind before I ever called you, so I might as well get on with it. Demary, I think I'm the one that gang was after when they kidnapped your secretary. I was in this building, you know.''

"What makes you think so? I know you look a lot like Martha but..."

"It isn't that. I mean, that's part of it, but the main thing is they tried again last night. The only reason I'm here right now is because my guy is a linebacker for the Seahawks. But anyway, one of them said something that got me thinking and I'm sure I'm right."

"What happened?''

"Remember I told you before that I had this crawly feeling like I was being watched all the time?''

I nodded.

"Well, right after I told you, it went away and I figured I'd been imagining things. Then, just the other day, it started again. And this time I made one of them. Lavander Starr.''

"Who's he?''

"He's a member of a gang called the New Janizarys. The gang was started by local talent but we think they've been taken over recently by an outside bunch. We're not sure where the new ones are from—we think the southwest, New Mexico or Texas. We had a tip on them about three weeks ago; they were supposed to have opened a new crack house, but when we got there it was clean. For me, though, the important thing is that Lavander was in the house when we busted the place, so he knows me by sight.''

"And you think he's been following you?'' I asked, wondering if I should tell her that Martha thought her kidnappers had been Janizarys.

"I know he's been following me; what I don't know is why. Whether it's personal, or connected with the Janizarys. But, anyway, to get back to last night.'' She looked down at her hands, twisting them back and forth in her lap. "I worked a different shift yesterday and I didn't get out of uniform until after six o'clock, so I called Frank, my date, and told him I'd meet him under the viaduct across from the Coleman ferry terminal instead of him picking me up at home. We were going to wander around and look through some of those shops on the dock for a while and then have dinner at a restaurant on the waterfront. I got there about seven, got out of my car, and was locking the door when I heard someone say, 'Are you sure it's the right broad this time?' and I knew he was talking about me.''

"Where were they? Or he? Did you see who it was?''

"No, but I felt them. I mean, I felt them coming

up behind me, and I knew I didn't have time to get back in the car. I jumped forward, between the next two cars, but I didn't have a chance of getting away. And then I saw Frank over by the terminal and screamed for all I was worth. Thank goodness he heard me. He was across the street in about thirty seconds flat.''

"Did he see them?''

"He saw them in the sense that he saw three men. They took off when they saw him coming. He couldn't describe them except to say that they were black and pretty good-sized.''

Jean was so nervous she was making me edgy, but I couldn't figure out what she was so uptight about. There was nothing in what she'd told me that should be making her that jumpy. Nor was there anything secret. I waited for her to go on but she had apparently finished.

"There's something else, isn't there?'' I asked her finally. "What? What you just described comes with the territory when you're a cop. You know that. You've got something else on your mind. What is it?''

"I think somebody on the force is in with the Janizarys,'' she whispered.

"Who?''

"That's just it. I don't know.''

"Well, if you don't know, what are you in such a sweat about? The idea that you've got a rogue cop on the force isn't anything new. Martha told me that a week ago."

She gaped at me. "Martha did? How does she know?"

"For heaven's sake, Jean. It's no big secret. Half of South Seattle knows someone is protecting the Janizarys." That was an exaggeration but it wasn't too far off the mark. "The big question is, who? Do you know?"

She hesitated, finally shaking her head no. "I've been working on it, though. On my own time. I've got some ideas but I haven't come up with anything positive yet."

"Have you talked to Internal Affairs? Or anyone else?"

"No. No one."

"Well, from the sound of it you'd better talk to someone and tell them what you do know, or suspect. If it was the Janizarys last night, and I think you're probably right about that, because Martha thought they were the ones who grabbed her, you need to tell your partner at least. And if I were you I'd tell Sam. I've known him forever and I can guarantee you he isn't bent. He's so straight-arrow, so clean, he squeaks."

"No. I can't—"

She was interrupted by the sound of the outside door opening. A moment later Martha came in.

She started to back out, apologizing for breaking in on us, but I told her to come on in.

I expected them to be startled by each other's looks, but when they were together they didn't look as much alike. Side by side the differences in their sizes and ages became more noticeable. There was just a strong resemblance between them. You could certainly see where one of them could be mistaken for the other if you were going only by a description, though, which was probably all the kidnappers had.

Martha listened to my abbreviated account of Jean's story and nodded her head.

"Of course, how stupid of me," she said. "I should have figured it out myself. That's what they said when they left me tied to that tree. Not the wrong *road,* the wrong *broad.*"

"Now, the next question is, how did they know you were here?" I asked Jean. "If they mistook Martha for you they couldn't have been following you. So how did they know?"

Jean gave me a sick look. "I had Harry Madison's business card, with our appointment date written on it, Scotch-taped to the inside of my locker door for nearly a month. I made the appointment so far in advance I was afraid I'd forget it. Anyone in the whole department could have seen the card when I had the door open.''

"Well, that pretty well solves that then, doesn't it?" I said.

We discussed the Janizarys for a while, trading ideas and trying to figure out why they had let Martha go, then Jean left.

Martha walked her to the door. When she came back she was frowning. "She didn't tell us everything she knows," she said flatly.

"No. You're right," I agreed. "But what didn't she tell us?"

"At a guess I'd say she has a good idea of who the bad cop is, but you don't shop your friends, you know. Especially if you aren't sure."

"She's a darn fool then. Whoever it is must be on to her. She's going to get herself killed."

Martha had a message from Helen. She had gotten the information I asked for from Barbara Johnson.

Karl had gone through the first six grades in Seattle and had then gone to the New Mexico Military Institute in Roswell. From there he went on to the University of Texas at El Paso.

"Barbara didn't think he had any local friends

left from grade school, and didn't think any of his other school friends, from New Mexico or Texas, lived in Seattle," Martha told me. "But she said you could check the desk in his apartment for names and addresses if you wanted to. She gave me the key. They took down the crime-scene tapes this morning. I went through the desk in his office but I didn't find anything personal at all."

She handed me a single key on a string.

"He had one old school friend here," I told her. "Or at least they went to school in El Paso at the same time. Howie Morgan. Sam told me."

"Maybe he knows."

"Knows what?"

"If there are any of their old schoolmates living around here. Why don't you ask him?" Martha asked.

I scowled at her. She knew I wouldn't ask Howie the time of day if I could help it.

"So—how did your day go?" I asked.

She'd had a couple of technical problems with the computer, which we discussed for a few minutes, but on the whole she had made pretty good progress. She hadn't uncovered anything we didn't already know but she thought she might have some fresh information for me by the next evening.

After she left I got started on the job that had come in the morning mail from Harbor Insurance. Harbor is a small, very old, very conservative firm that keeps C.R.I. not only solvent, but in the black. At least once a month they send me the names of anywhere from one to five persons they want located, dead or alive. Literally. Policyholders who had not paid their premiums for some time. What happened after I located them I don't know, but as Harbor paid well and quickly, I did their work the same way.

I spent about an hour getting the preliminaries down and then decided to knock off for the day. It was still early—not yet six o'clock—so I headed back down the freeway to see what I could find in Karl's apartment.

SIXTEEN

SEATTLE IS a beautiful city at any time, but when the weather is just right it is gorgeous. Today was one of the gorgeous days. The ragged, snow-capped peaks of the Cascade Mountains marched along the skyline on my left, Puget Sound sparkled on my right, and in between all the downtown high-rise buildings were glittering in the sunlight like so many diamonds. It was a picture-postcard afternoon.

Snarled as it is with interstate highway construction, Seattle also has some of the worst traffic problems I know of. It took me nearly two hours to get from the center of town to the Renton off-ramp, a distance that normally took less than ten minutes. Not only was the traffic horrendous, a produce truck had slewed around sideways and dumped its load on the freeway just north of the old Boeing airport. The resulting mess closed three of the four southbound lanes. There were tomatoes, lettuce, and zucchini all over the place. The highway could have doubled for a tossed salad.

My watch showed eight-thirty by the time I got

to Karl's apartment building in a newish development behind the Renton Center Mall. The location made me wonder how well Karl had known the waitress. The place wasn't all that easy to find.

I was thinking about the waitress when I unlocked the door to Karl's apartment and stepped into the entryway, so it was several seconds before what I saw actually registered on my brain.

Someone had searched the place. There was no really obvious mess, nothing thrown around or trashed, but if you knew anything at all you could see that it had been gone over, thoroughly, and not by the Seattle PD. They do a different kind of job, and they don't make any effort to cover up what they've done. Whoever had done this had not had much experience and had tried to hide his work.

I was still standing in the little hall looking through into the living room when it dawned on me that maybe the reason it looked like it did was because he, whoever he was, wasn't finished yet. The thought that he might still be there, in one of the other rooms, or just around the corner of the wall, gave me a fast adrenaline jolt.

I backed out a lot quicker than I'd gone in. No one dashed out to grab me and I didn't hear anything, but I didn't feel the least bit foolish about retreating either.

I drove back to the mall and called Sam—at home—from a corner telephone booth. He listened to my story, asked me exactly where I was, and told me to stay there until the Renton PD arrived. He'd call them. Then he proceeded to call me all kinds of a fool and demanded to know why I didn't stay home where I belonged. I couldn't believe it. He knew I was unnerved, frightened, and he yelled at me anyway. Which maybe was the right thing to do. At any rate, when we hung up I was over my scare; I was so mad I was shaking.

I was still mad at him forty-five minutes later when he arrived to take a look at the apartment for himself. I had already gone over the place with the Renton men so I thought about just stalking off and leaving him to it, but I was afraid I couldn't carry it off. I'm not good at grand gestures.

He didn't speak to me at all.

The Renton men had pulled up beside my phone booth within minutes. I gave them the key, told them where the apartment was, and, at their request, followed them back there. They checked the apartment out and found it empty, then called me inside to answer questions.

They wanted to know whose apartment it was, what I was doing there, where I had gotten the key, all that sort of thing, but it was mostly just to fill out their report. As far as they were concerned, this particular crime was part of a Seattle homicide so the Seattle boys could have it.

I didn't blame them. Break-ins are a real pain to solve if the perp doesn't immediately try to peddle whatever he takes.

And it *was* a break-in. The back door had been forced, but there was no way of telling what the guy had been after, if he had found it, or even if the break-in was connected with Karl's death. Although one thing did strike me. Whatever he had been looking for, it hadn't been small. None of the cushions had been slashed, none of the drawers had been dumped, and no small things, such as the canisters on the kitchen counter, were out of place. At a guess, I'd say he, or they, had been looking for something at least as large as a bread box.

The Renton men had called Barbara Johnson. She got there a few minutes before Sam did, but she couldn't help much. She said there was nothing obvious missing, like the TV or any of his paintings. One of which she said was quite valuable, an unsigned trompe l'oeil attributed to William Harnett, a late nineteenth-century still-life painter. On the other hand she had been gone for six weeks and didn't know what he might have acquired while she was away.

Sam took over when he arrived. He had a lab team right behind him, so the Renton men left. Barbara stood and talked to me for a few minutes, then she too left. I accompanied her to the door, meaning to keep right on going, but Sam stopped me and told me to go wait in the little dining room.

What he actually said was: "Jones, go sit down in the dining room, and stay there until I tell you you can go."

"Stick it in your ear," I said rudely, and walked on out.

Somebody snickered.

Sam caught me in the hall, grabbing my arm so hard it hurt.

"Listen, Demary," he hissed at me. "You get back in there and wait until I have a chance to talk to you. You hear me?"

I was so surprised I didn't say a word. He was furious at me, really angry. He's been mad at me plenty of times, but this was different. I'd never seen him like that.

I followed him back into the apartment and sat down at the dining room table to do some heavy thinking.

There was something very strange about the way Sam was acting, and not just at the moment either, but for several days. It had started a week ago with the row we'd had in McRory's over Deke Long. A row that had simmered all week and seemed to come to a boil every so often.

I thought back, trying to see some kind of a pattern, but there was nothing I could put my finger on. The two biggest fights we'd had involved Deke Long but after thinking about those two battles for a while I realized he was riled up before either of the arguments even started. And the same thing was true of tonight. He was already uptight when he had answered the phone this evening. My call had simply been the spark that set him off.

Something was really bothering Sam. Something serious.

Almost everyone else had gone home by eleven-thirty, and I'd been waiting well over an hour before he wanted to talk to me. Then all he did was ask me some unimportant questions that didn't have any bearing on the present situation at all. Afterward he walked me to my car.

He also followed me home.

SEVENTEEN

MARTHA CALLED ME from Great Western at ten-thirty the next morning. And lit into me without even bothering to say hello.

"Are you crazy, Demary?" she demanded. "What are you playing at?"

"For Pete's sake. Not you too," I grumbled. "Sam already yelled at me last night. You don't have to do it again."

"I just can't believe you'd do anything so bloody stupid. It's a wonder you didn't get yourself killed. Why didn't you tell me you were going to Karl's apartment last night? I'd have gone with you at least."

"Then both of us could have gotten killed." I said, sounding sour even to myself. "The thing is, it just never occurred to me that it might be dangerous. Whoever killed Karl had all night to search the place last Friday while he was there; why come back?"

"Then you do think Karl's killer was in there last night?"

"Well, not necessarily, but surely somebody who is a part of the whole thing."

"Barbara said the Renton PD thought it was simply a break-in and you scared them off."

"Yes, maybe they do, but I don't. For one thing, nothing was taken. He, or they, were searching for something specific, and something fairly large." I went on to tell her how the apartment looked.

"You think they were trying to find the last cocaine shipment?"

"That's my guess. Peter Johnson didn't say what he'd done with the two cases he found, but I don't think he left them where he found them."

"No, but I doubt if he'd take them over to Karl's place either. At that point he was suspicious of Karl."

"True, but you and I are the only people who know that. I still haven't told Sam or anyone else what he wanted me to do."

"When you get right down to it, if it wasn't a random break-in, it doesn't make sense," Martha said slowly. "Unless, and this is pure pie-in-the-sky guessing, unless there are two people involved at command level. Two head men. One or both of whom are making independent moves."

"I suppose that's possible. It doesn't seem too likely, but..."

"It might explain why so many offbeat things have happened," Martha said thoughtfully. "Things that don't fit."

"What things?"

"Well, for starters, my being kidnapped at exactly the same time Peter Johnson was shot. It almost had to have been coincidental. No one would plan it that way. And last night. If whoever tossed Karl's place wasn't his killer, what was he looking for? If it was the killer, why didn't he search the place when he was there to start with?"

"If you think of it that way, it doesn't make much sense."

"Not unless someone is really playing silly."

On that note Martha rang off. I went back to work studying the personnel records she had brought me the day before. However, after a few minutes I gave up on them and pushed the file aside. I kept thinking about what she'd said, about so many things being out of kilter, off-center somehow.

The same thought had gone through my mind a dozen times but I'd never focused on the two-person—or two-group—possibility. Some of the strange bits weren't so strange viewed from that perspective. The MOs of the three killings—I was including Deke Long—were so different there could easily be two separate groups involved.

It was an interesting thought.

Karl's murder seemed to be a pretty straightforward piece of work, the only question being who had done the killing. Peter Johnson's murder wasn't as simple. If they had been killed by two different people it would solve a lot. There were still a number of unanswered questions, though. The one that continued to stick in my mind like a burr was Peter Johnson's appointment with me on Tuesday afternoon.

How had the killer known about it?

And how had he known the window in the Alhambra hallway overlooked my door? The building was not open to the public. Did he live in the building now; had he ever lived there?

I left the office early, thinking I might go find Joey. Past tenants were something he could check on. He saved me the trouble of looking for him. Dressed in a pair of torn jeans, and a T-shirt that I'd be willing to bet a five-spot his mother hadn't purchased—the sentiment scrawled across his skinny chest was not only vulgar, it was obscene— he was leaning up against the rear fender of my car when I turned around after locking the office door.

"Joey. Good. I was looking for you," I said, trying to keep my eyes off his shirt.

"I don't have anything to report but thought I'd check in," he said, elaborately casual. "See how you were making out. Any progress?"

"Uh, well, no. Not really. No progress, but I've got something else I want you to do for me. Okay?"

"Sure. What do you need?"

"I want to know how Peter Johnson's killer knew the window in the Alhambra overlooked my doorway. See what you can find out about the people who live in the building, or have lived there in the past, or anyone who is a regular visitor. Be careful; the police have checked out the tenants but that doesn't mean the killer isn't still around."

Joey shook his head. "He's not living there now. I know every tenant. But it could be someone who used to live there. I'll get my crew right on it."

Calling to someone across the street, he pushed himself away from the fender in a flying leap, and tore off down the street before I could stop him.

"Tomorrow," he hollered at me. "I'll catch you tomorrow."

"Joey, wait!" I yelled.

He paid no attention and in a second was out of sight.

"Darn," I muttered, staring after him. What crew was he talking about? If he or one of his little pals got into trouble... Talking to his cohorts was one thing. I didn't want him questioning the tenants, or any other adults.

Cass picked me up at seven that evening. He had reservations for dinner and a show. I didn't enjoy it as much as I should have. I was back where I'd been a couple of days before, somehow uncomfortable when I was with him. There wasn't any reason for the way I felt and it made me furious with myself. Despite my unease it was a nice evening, though; no riotous fun, but nice. We ended up at the Canoe House again and a few minutes after we got there Sam came in. The Canoe House seemed to be one of his regular ports of call too. Either that or he was following me again.

Cass signaled to him to join us.

I had been telling Cass about the computer file Peter Johnson had left, and after the waitress delivered Sam's drink, I finished the story.

"So what did he do with the marked case? Or cases?" Cass asked, looking at me and then Sam. "What happened to the cocaine?"

"We don't know," I told him. "He didn't say."

"Have you searched the warehouse?" he asked Sam.

"More or less."

"What do you mean, more or less?" I asked. The phrase didn't sound like Sam. And as a matter of fact, he wasn't acting like himself either. The difference was fairly subtle; Cass didn't seem to be picking up on it, but I certainly could. I couldn't tell what was causing it, though. For a minute or so I wondered if he might be jealous of Cass, but decided that was silly.

"The warehouse is a big place," Sam said with a shrug. "Pretty hard to do a really good job on it, and I don't think he'd hide it there anyway."

Cass gave him a speculative look but he didn't say anything.

"Why not?" I asked, somewhat obstinately. "He must have known the place pretty thoroughly. Plus the fact that the night watchman didn't see him carrying any cases out of there."

"How do you know that?" Sam demanded, frowning at me.

"I asked him."

"What the heck are you doing interrogating a witness?" Sam yelled.

I was so surprised I just stared at him. Cass said something, trying to smooth things over, but I didn't hear what it was. Sam jumped up, knocking his chair over in the process, and stomped out without answering him.

Cass looked after him and then back at me. "What in tarnation was that all about?" he asked. "Has he been chewing locoweed?"

"I don't know," I said, quite honestly. "He's been mad at me for a week, and I don't know why. I've got a perfect right to talk to Dave, and Sam knows it."

"I hate to be nosy, sugar," Cass drawled. "But who in the heck is Dave? And what was he a witness to?"

"He's the night watchman at Great Western," I said, surprised that he didn't know. We had never happened to talk about the man, but Cass had been in Sam's office the afternoon Helen Wagoner called Sam and told him about the night watchman.

"Well, yes, I was there when Miss Wagoner called," Cass said, when I asked him. "But I think I was just leaving when the call came and I guess I never did ask what she had to say."

I told him what Dave had seen, and how it tied into Peter Johnson's computer file.

"Doesn't hardly seem important enough to yell

at you for,'' he said, grinning at me. His turquoise blue eyes twinkled. ''I think Sam's jealous.''

''Well, if he is, he's got no business being so,'' I said, annoyed. I didn't think Cass had any business sounding so smug either, and I let him know it. As a result, we finished our drinks and left without having much more to say to each other.

When we got to the parking lot I saw Sam's car across the street. He followed us home.

I didn't say anything to Cass, and I don't know if he spotted Sam or not, but he let me out in front of my house a few minutes after eleven with a less-than-loverly ''good night.'' Which suited me fine. By that time I was royally ticked off at both of them.

EIGHTEEN

THE PHONE WOKE ME at seven the next morning. It was Sam. His disposition hadn't changed any since I'd talked to him last, but at least he had a better reason for acting like a grizzly with a sore paw.

Dave Porter, the Great Western night watchman we'd had the disagreement about, had been killed in a freak accident sometime between nine and one the night before.

Sam wanted me downtown, now, if not sooner.

"You woke me up," I told him. "What do you want me for anyway? I don't know anything."

"You got that right," he said sourly. "I want to know when you talked to him, what he said, what you said, all of it. And knowing you, you've got it on your computer, so bring me a printout."

I could have told him to stuff it; I didn't have to report to him or anyone else, but I was beginning to worry about him. I've known Sam a long time, and despite our differences, and recent squabbles, I like him. At times I guess it's been more than liking, but whatever, something was giving him a hard time and I didn't need to add to his problems. I told him I'd be down as soon as I could, and hung up.

I took my time, however, having a cup of coffee and a hot shower before I pulled on an old pair of jeans and a sweatshirt. I wanted to try a little experiment on my way to town that might require some climbing.

I was going to follow pal Joey's suggestion and see if I could get into the Alhambra through the basement of an apartment on Forty-sixth, without being challenged.

Joey was right. I could and I did, and without the least bit of trouble. I parked in a private driveway on Forty-seventh, walked down the alley to Forty-sixth, across the street, and into the first building I came to. The door not only wasn't locked, it was propped open with a stack of bricks. I could hear a vacuum going in the upstairs hall.

The door to the basement was at the back of the ground-floor entry hall and had a small cardboard sign taped to the center panel with the words LAUNDRY ROOM printed on it with a Magic Marker.

Downstairs, I found three windows that gave easy access to the enclosed space between the buildings. One in the hall and two in the laundry. All of them slid open easily. I used the one in the hall, climbed out, and trotted over to the back door of the Alhambra, also standing wide open, and went up to the second floor. All without seeing a soul.

There was no one in the hall either, nor in the alcove containing the window that looked out on my office.

The alcove was actually part of the fire exit, the fire door being at a right angle to the window. The way the window was placed the killer could have stood there indefinitely, waiting for Peter Johnson to show himself, without ever having to worry about being seen.

The whole trip was so easy, in and out of both buildings and back to my car, it was almost funny.

Which didn't stop Sam from scowling at me when I told him about the experiment a half hour later.

"Demary, haven't you been listening to me at all?" he asked. "Five people, and possibly six, have been murdered in this case so far. Have you got a death wish or something? Do you want to be number seven?"

"Six? Who's number six? Not Dave? You said it was an accident."

"It will go down on the books as an accident, but I don't think it was."

"Well, are you going to tell me what happened, or do I have to guess?"

"You knew he got back from Denver yesterday, and that he lives in an apartment?"

At my nod, he went on. "Well, it looks like he was taking his suitcases down to the storage room in the basement, somehow tripped over them, and fell down the stairs. The stairs and the floor are concrete. He was found at the bottom, sprawled upside down with one of the suitcases under him. His neck was broken and he had a number of bruises consistent with such a fall."

For a second I had an eerie feeling of déjà vu, but I couldn't place what caused it.

"But why?" I asked. "Why was he killed? He wasn't a threat to anyone. He had already told all he knew to Helen, me, you, and whoever it was you had talk to him in Denver."

Sam shook his head. "I don't know why. I wish to heck I did. On the face of it there isn't any reason for his death but I'm still sure he's number six."

He didn't say anything for a minute, then he leaned forward over his desk and took my hand. "Demary, leave it alone," he said in a pleading tone. "You're darn good at what you do but that doesn't include tracking down a multiple killer.

You go ramming around climbing through basement windows and I'm going to find you dead somewhere.''

I pulled my hand away slowly, touched in spite of myself. Sam seemed a bit more relaxed than he'd been earlier in the day, or for several days. We talked for a while like we always had before, just kicking things around. He told me Howie had been working on the case too whenever he had the time. Howie had been working the two-to-ten shift for the past three days, however, so he hadn't been able to accomplish much.

Personally I didn't have much faith in Howie accomplishing anything regardless, but I didn't say so. I was just glad that whatever had been bugging Sam seemed to have eased off.

NINETEEN

AFTER I LEFT SAM'S OFFICE I drove uptown to the Pike Place Market on First and Pike. I found a parking space immediately—a small miracle around the market—and spent the next hour enjoying myself, weaving my way through the crowds around the vegetable stalls, checking out the fresh fish stands, taking in the tantalizing scents and sounds of the market. I bought crunchy-crisp Bibb lettuce, tomatoes, radishes, and a half-dozen other salad fixings as well as a fresh-cooked Dungeness crab. I stopped at Market Spice to buy one of their special seasonings, Green Magic, then walked over to DeLaurenti's International Market on the corner. DeLaurenti's has a fabulous selection of imported foods, and they also sell the best sourdough French bread I've ever eaten.

On my way back I spotted Jean Clausen going into one of the eating establishments that look out over the Sound from the back of the market. I went ahead and left my sacks full of goodies in the car (on top of everything else I'd bought garlic-cured Spanish olives and two different kinds of cheese to go with my crab feed), and then returned to the restaurant to see what Jean was up to.

I expected some kind of a welcome, I mean, at least a semi-friendly "hello," but Jean wasn't pleased to see me and she made that very clear. I think she thought if she could make me uncomfortable enough I'd leave. She didn't know me very well. After a minute or so, when she saw it wasn't working, she gave up and introduced me to the young man she had with her. He was several years her junior.

"Demary, this is Larry Nichols," she said. "He's Howie Morgan's partner."

I hate it when I act like a nerd, but I couldn't help grinning. Whoever had arranged that pairing must have had a sense of humor. Howie is tall, dark-haired, slender, and a complete sophisticate. Larry Nichols looked like Huck Finn's kid brother. He was short and overweight, with a round, freckled face, straw-blond hair, soft blue eyes, and the longest eyelashes I've ever seen outside a box.

"Larry and I just got off work," Jean told me.

Larry gave her a surprised look but he didn't say anything.

"How long have you been Howie's partner?" I

asked him, taking a sip of the chicory-flavored coffee I'd stopped to get on the way in.

"Ever since we got out of training," he said. "Well, I was with Spokes for a while, but then Howie and I got together."

He made it sound as if both he and Howie had been working toward that end, which, knowing Howie, I didn't believe. I also knew he hadn't just gotten off work. Sam had told me less than an hour ago that Howie was working the two-to-ten evening shift.

Larry and Jean had apparently been talking about the Peter Johnson killing and after a few minutes Jean steered him back to the subject with a question about his shifts that week.

"Howie and I were on days all week," he told her. "Twelve till eight at night."

"Oh? Where were you when Peter Johnson got shot?" Jean asked. "Why didn't you answer the call? It's your beat."

Larry looked uncomfortable. "Well, uh, to tell the truth we were off the air."

"Off the air? Why? Where were you?" Jean pressed. "Where was Howie?"

Larry glanced at me nervously. "Look, I don't think... I don't know..."

"Oh, for heaven's sake, Larry, Demary's all

right," Jean said impatiently. "What are you trying to cover up?"

"Cover up? I'm not trying to c...cover up anything," Larry stuttered, bewildered by Jean's suddenly sharp tone. "We were parked in front of the Boys' Club on Forty-fifth and Stoneway. I was, anyway. Howie was inside. It's just... It's just that Howie doesn't want anyone to know we're building up our own string of snitches. He says the brass will say we haven't been on the street long enough. That's what he was doing in the Boys' Club. Talking to one of our snitches about a B&E."

"How long was he in there?" I asked. I couldn't quite figure what Jean was after, what she thought they were into.

"About fifteen minutes, I think," he said. "He couldn't find P...uh, our guy. He went in there about one-thirty. I'm not positive about the time because I broke my watch that morning, but I know we answered another call at one-fifty-six."

"Is your snitch a kid?"

"Uh, well, yes. A teenager."

Nobody said anything for a moment; we all knew the department frowned on using teenagers as snitches. Then Jean changed the subject by asking him how he'd broken his watch.

Larry gave an embarrassed little laugh. "Actually, I didn't. Howie did. He didn't mean to, of course, but he insisted on buying me a new one.'' He held out his wrist. ''Nice, isn't it? I told him to forget it, the one I had was an el cheapo, but he bought this one for me anyway.''

The watch was a expensive brand. Made me wonder if I'd been wrong about Howie. People do choose strange friends sometimes.

''How did he happen to break your old one?'' Jean gave the new one an admiring inspection.

''Just an accident. It happened that morning. He knocked it off the bench and stepped on it. I'd taken it off when I was changing into my uniform. My fault, really. I shouldn't have left it there.''

Jean took a gulp of her coffee and gazed out over the water. She suddenly looked tired and dispirited. Whatever it was she had hoped to learn from Larry apparently hadn't materialized.

''I was raised in Kansas,'' Larry said abruptly. ''Back home, when I was a kid, I was afraid of the water. Rivers and things. I didn't know it could be so…so beautiful.'' He waved at the scene framed in the window beside us.

Covered with sun-sparked whitecaps, the choppy water of Puget Sound looked like a field of daisies. Dozens of small sailboats were flash-dancing across the waves. Below us, one of the big

Alaska ferries came into its dock trailing a glittering welter of froth and foam.

I finished my coffee and left. I would have liked to stay and see if I could persuade Jean to tell me what she knew, or thought she knew, but I sensed it wouldn't do any good. For whatever reason, she was still determined to keep it to herself.

The downtown traffic was terrible, as usual, so it was getting late by the time I stopped at the office on my way home. I needed to catch up on the mail. With Martha gone it was piling up. There wasn't anything important in it, but there was a pleasant letter from Mr. X. Along with enclosing a check, he thanked me and said he was pleased with the way I'd done the job, and also said he had recommended me to several of his friends who were interested in buying investment paintings. That was good to hear. Actually, I had enjoyed tracing the provenance of his picture. Sam would like my doing that kind of work too. It was nice and safe, provided, of course, I didn't go sticking my pointy little nose into areas that had nothing to do with the art world.

When I got home my answering machine had two calls on it. One from Cass saying he would call me later, and one from Joey telling me to call him immediately.

Even on the answering machine Joey sounded excited. And once I talked to him I didn't blame him. He had found three eyewitnesses—*three*—to Martha's kidnapping.

TWENTY

JOEY ANSWERED on the first ring. He must have been sitting beside the phone. He could hardly wait to tell me his news.

"I got three sets of eyes who saw what happened to the black fox," he told me, his voice squeaking with excitement.

"How old are they?" I asked, after I deciphered what he'd said.

"Jake's twelve and his sister Ellen is nine. And they know what they saw," he assured me. "I don't know about their mother, Mrs. Fields, but she acts pretty sensible. She should be able to tell a straight story."

"Their mother saw it too? Why hasn't she gone to the police?" I asked, still half expecting some kind of a negative punch line.

"Jake says he never knew the cops were looking for witnesses, so she probably didn't either. I ain't talked to her myself. I figured you'd want to question her firsthand."

"Yeah. Right," I agreed.

Joey rattled off the Fields' house number, told

me how to get there, and said he'd let Jake know I was on my way.

He hung up before I thought to tell him I didn't want him—or his crew—talking to the tenants of the Alhambra.

Mrs. Fields was expecting me. I don't know what her son Jake had told her, she seemed to be secretly amused about something, but she asked me in anyway.

"I'm sorry I didn't contact you, or the police," she said, after she had checked my ID. "But until Jake explained that the woman had been kidnapped, not arrested, I had no idea anything was wrong. Nor did Jake until Joey told him."

"Arrested? I'm sorry... I don't..."

"Here, won't you sit down?" she asked, gesturing toward the couch in front of the windows. "Would you like a cup of coffee? I just made a pot of Starbucks."

"I'd love a cup, thanks," I said, sitting down a bit carefully. A really huge and very unfriendly-looking cat was curled up on the far end of the couch. I couldn't help wondering if I wasn't on a futile errand. It didn't sound as if Mrs. Fields was talking about Martha at all. However, Joey had never failed me yet, so I sat and waited while Mrs. Fields went for the coffee. Returning, she handed me a steaming mug, asked if I wanted anything in it, and pulled a chair around for herself.

"Yes. The three men who took her to the car were wearing some kind of uniform. I just assumed they were police and didn't think any more about it," she said.

This was something new. Martha had not seen any uniforms. "Where were you? How far away were you?" I asked, still not sure she had seen Martha.

"We were coming out of the drugstore. We were just outside the door when we saw them, so I guess we must have been about thirty or forty feet away from your office door."

"Well, if you don't mind, would you think back to just before you left the drugstore, and tell me as exactly as you can everything you saw. Or heard."

Mrs. Fields thought for a moment, and then nodded briskly. "Yes. All right. But first you have to understand we were going, or going to go, in the opposite direction, away from your office, so I only caught a quick look at what happened. Also the kids were arguing and squabbling about something and I was more interested in stopping their bickering than I was in anything else that was going on. As we stepped out onto the sidewalk I heard what I thought was a child screaming somewhere in the distance and at almost the same time a truck started backfiring. The street was noisy with cars besides so I practically yelled at Jake to get on the other side of me, to separate the two of them, and as we kind of milled around the three men came out of your building with the woman.''

She stopped, gazing vacantly at a spot somewhere over my head, apparently consulting her memory. In a minute she went on.

''I was trying to remember what was odd about them and I think it was her feet. At the time I thought the men were policemen and that she was being arrested, but even then I noticed that something wasn't quite right. They came out of the building very quickly and had her in the car almost immediately, but now that I think about it her feet weren't on the ground. She wasn't actually walking. Her arms were bent and they were carrying her by her elbows. I thought then that she was resisting arrest or something and that they were hustling her into the car before she could cause them any more trouble, but…it happened so fast I didn't pay all that much attention. I'm sorry I can't remember more.''

''You're doing fine,'' I assured her. ''I'm surprised you even saw that much because, as you say, they must have been moving pretty fast. Can you describe them, or anyone of them?''

She thought about that for another minute and then shook her head regretfully. ''No, I can't. Not really. They were all black, and I have the impression that they were large, but it's just an impression.''

''How about the uniforms they were wearing? Can you tell me anything about them? The color, any insignia, anything?''

''They were dark blue. I guess that's why I thought they were policemen. And they had hats on like the police wear, with bills. And yes, one of them did have an insignia on his sleeve, a large round patch of red and white check.''

''Did you see anything or anyone else that struck you as being different, out of the ordinary?''

''No, not really. Although I do realize now the backfiring I heard must have been the shots that were fired at you. Also I guess I saw the woman who first realized what had happened. She walked past us as we started up the street. I did notice her running back toward the drugstore just as we turned the corner but I didn't pay her any notice because she wasn't calling out or anything, and we were a half block away by that time.''

I continued to talk to Mrs. Fields for another ten

minutes or so but she didn't have anything useful
to add. When I asked, she called the girl, Ellen, in
from the yard so I could talk to her, and later called
Jake from his room where he was watching TV.

They both, separately, added a few minor de-
scriptive details on the three men, but the total
wasn't enough to form an identification. What the
boy, Jake, did do, though, was positively identify
Martha. He had seen her in the office and knew
her personally from having sold her Boy Scout
Clamorama tickets.

I told Mrs. Fields I'd notify the police and that
she and the two kids would have to repeat their
stories for them, but an officer would probably
come to the house. They wouldn't have to go to
the station. That disappointed Jake; he said he had
been looking forward to the trip downtown and to
seeing what a real police department looked like.

I made a mental note to see if Sam couldn't
arrange a ride for him in a black-and-white, and
told them good-bye.

I was in a hurry to call Martha so I stopped at
the office rather than going on home. It was nearly
four o'clock and I knew she and Charles were going to Olympia for some kind of academic do at
the capitol. They would be leaving any minute, if
they hadn't done so already, and I wanted her re-

action to the Fields' story. I thought it might trigger her memory.

It did.

"A proper idiot I am," she said disgustedly. "I should have remembered that patch. It was undoubtedly what made me think they were part of the New Janizarys. About a week before this all started there was a picture in the paper of two of the Janizary gang members who work at that fancy car wash on Rainier Avenue. You know, the one where they serve you a glass of nonalcoholic wine while you're waiting for your car. All the employees wear some kind of uniform. I've forgotten why these two were in the paper, but they were picked up at work and still had their uniforms on in the picture. The outfits are navy blue, and do look something like a police uniform, with a big red and white check thing on the sleeve. I saw that arm patch when I was wrestling with them in the hall."

"Well, at least we know that much for sure now. And I guess we can also be sure they were after Jean, not you. I still can't figure out why they let you go like they did, though."

"I've got a guess."

"You have? What?"

"It's nothing more than just that, a guess, but I've been thinking about it and they may have let me go for almost the same reason they killed Peter Johnson. I don't think they wanted Peter Johnson talking to you because they, or he, is afraid of you. Or maybe I should say, afraid of what you might find out if you got on the right track. And they may have let me go because they plain and simple didn't want you coming after them as you might do if they offed me.''

"That's crazy," I protested. "You're making me sound like Sherlock Holmes or something.''

"No, not that, definitely not that. I think it's someone who knows you personally, and knows what a pain you can be. Or to put it less elegantly, knows you're so bullheaded you'd never give up.''

With that, she hung up before I could answer.

TWENTY-ONE

THERE WAS ANOTHER CALL from Cass on my answering machine when I got back to the house. He called again while I was stuffing myself with fresh crab—it's no wonder I'm a little overweight—but I left the machine on and didn't answer. I was still ticked off at him. I didn't want to see him or talk to him.

After I finished eating I cleaned up the kitchen— as opposed to just shoving the dishes in the dishwasher. I'd had a sharp note from Nora concerning the condition I'd left it in the day before. When I was done I changed into jeans again, having put on a decent pair of slacks to go talk to Mrs. Fields. Getting ready this time included sticking my ID in one boot, and some bills in the other. I was going back downtown.

I put a handful of change and a stack of pictures I'd had printed into the pocket of the old army fatigue jacket I wore and I was ready.

Most of the street people I knew as a kid were someplace else now. Some had graduated to bigger if not necessarily better things; some, like myself, realized they were making a mistake and got out; some had simply disappeared, but there were still a few around that I knew. One of these was a woman now well into her sixties who went by the name of Markie.

Markie was a panhandler. She worked the Pike Place Market, which was probably where her name came from, and it was she I'd gone to the market to find that morning. I'd spotted her on my first walk-through and had let her know I wanted to talk to her later. Saturday was Markie's biggest day; I knew better than to take up any of her time right then.

Markie only worked the daylight hours but this time of year that meant until about eight o'clock. After that she went home to a bed-sitter in a rat trap of a hotel on Second Avenue that she had graduated to a number of years ago. Previously she had lived in a cardboard box arrangement under the viaduct. Now she stayed inside at night, not venturing out until morning. She was afraid of the streets at night now. She didn't welcome evening guests either but I'd been there before and she'd nodded reluctantly when I'd told her I'd be there tonight.

Markie was a lot like Joey. She wanted to know everything that was going on, and because she was more friendly than most of her kind, she knew a lot of the kids on the street.

And one of those kids might have what I was looking for. A description or a name.

No matter how I tried to work around it, the main stumbling block to any solution I came up with was always my appointment with Peter Johnson. How had the killer known about it at all, and how had he known about it in time to set up a hit?

I'd done a lot of thinking on the subject and I'd come to the conclusion that Karl had to be the informant. Maybe not purposely, but he did seem to be the only possible source of the information. The most likely time for him to have given it to anyone was Monday night. And the most likely person for him to have given it to was his dinner partner. The man who had called him Monday morning.

I'd asked Helen again if she'd remembered the man's name, but she was now fairly certain that he hadn't identified himself. However, Karl had told his father that they were going to the Fractured Goose, a somewhat strange choice for a young man of Karl's means and personality. The Fractured Goose wasn't a dive, but it was shabby and the clientele was on the rough side. There had to be a particular reason for Karl to have gone to the

Goose, and I was betting the reason was the other man had deliberately chosen the place because he didn't think Karl would be known there.

The Fractured Goose was north of Pioneer Square, several blocks from where most of the street kids hung out, but not so far away they didn't drift down there occasionally.

The clerk was asleep behind the desk when I walked into the lobby of Markie's apartment-hotel. The place smelled stale and sour, with an overriding reek of marijuana.

Markie lived on the second floor at the back of the building. She answered my knock and after assuring herself I was who I said I was, she let me in.

The room was stuffy and overwarm—it faced west and got the direct sun in the afternoon—but it was reasonably clean and uncluttered. Her bed was in a small alcove to the right of the door with some kind of a hot-plate arrangement in a curtained niche between it and the door to the bathroom. The main area contained an old overstuffed chair in front of the window, a TV, a small Formica-topped table with two unmatched straight chairs, and a chest of drawers. A mayonnaise jar full of pink carnations sat on top of the chest.

''Good to see you again, Demary,'' she said in

her soft voice, waving me toward one of the chairs by the table. From there she had a nice view of the corner of a small park on the waterfront. "Are you doing all right?"

"Yes, fine," I assured her. Knowing Markie, I knew she really cared how I was. "How are things for you?"

"Tolerably well. Arthritis is beginning to bother me some. I can't work much anymore when it's cold out, but that's the way it is when you get older."

I sat down and concealed the smile Markie's attitude toward her "work" always brought to my face. She considered herself a respectable, hardworking woman, and had no truck, as she called it, with those who lined up for a welfare handout. Markie's set of values may have been different than the norm, but within them she was the most honest person I knew.

She had tea already made and after pouring me a cup she asked me what I wanted this time. Markie had done odd jobs for me in the past.

"I need to find out who this man had dinner with on Monday night, the sixth of July. They were at the Fractured Goose," I said, handing her the stack of small pictures I'd had printed up from a studio portrait of Karl. Martha had borrowed it from his mother. "I'll pay for the name, or a good description."

Markie looked at the topmost picture. "What did he do?"

"He didn't do anything. He was killed, and the man he had dinner with that night may have had something to do with his death, or may know something that could lead to his killer."

"Two weeks ago, almost. Hard for most of them kids out there to remember what happened yesterday."

"I know, but it's worth a try. And some of them do hang out down around the Goose."

"How much is it worth to you?"

"For you? Our regular price. Fifty. For whoever has the information, whatever you think is fair. No more than another fifty, though."

Markie nodded. "Well, I'll pass 'em around. Talk to some of the older girls. See if anybody remembers him."

"And one other thing. A guy named Deke Long was killed in an alley off Occidental two nights later. Wednesday night. I'll pay for anything anybody knows about that too."

Markie frowned. "Snooping around killings is dangerous, Demary. You never done that before. How come you're into that kind of stuff?"

I told her about Peter Johnson and Karl's deaths and my getting shot.

"Bad, that's bad," she said, fingering the five twenties I'd put on the arm of her chair. "Might not be able to get anybody to talk for that price if they know about the killings."

I got up and made ready to leave. "I'll pay more, but only if you're sure it's a straight story. Okay?" I wasn't worried about the money. Markie's sense of what was right didn't include cheating a friend.

"Yes. All right. I'll see what I can do." She got up and started unbolting the door. "You be careful, Demary. You ain't no Sam Spade."

I SPENT THE NEXT couple of hours, until after eleven, drifting up and down First Avenue. I had five offers of employment and a lot of obscene suggestions before I finally found someone who was willing to talk to me.

A kid. A tall, thin boy with stringy brown hair who didn't look old enough to be on the street at all, let alone begging for crumbs to stay alive. He needed a fix, and for a price was willing to listen to my questions.

He wanted his money up front, said he had the

shakes too bad to concentrate, but I told him to forget it. Talk first, money second.

"I'm in bad shape," he whined, eyeing me furtively.

"You'll be in a whole lot worse shape if you try to take me," I assured him. "I had a brown belt before you were born." I didn't have anything of the kind, but he couldn't know that and I guess I looked tough to him. Attitude is everything on the street.

"What kind of information?" he muttered.

"I want to know where you're getting your stuff."

"You crazy?" He backed off and peered at me through red-rimmed eyes. "You a narc? I ain't tellin' you—"

"No, no, wait a minute," I interrupted. "I don't want names, I just want to know if there's plenty around. Can you get it anywhere? Everywhere? Is there a good supply, or has it been tight lately? How good has your supply been the last couple of weeks?"

"It ain't," he said, sudden anger in his tone. "It ain't been good at all. Half the time my main man ain't even got any; he wants more for it, and he's been cutting it again too. He says one of the big pipes is closed down. But there's fresh coming in soon. Soon.''

The pain, and fear, and want in his face was almost obscene. I felt sorry for him but I knew better than to offer anything other than the twenty I handed him.

He looked surprised—maybe he thought I'd want more for my money—and took off immediately, before I could change my mind. Halfway down the block he disappeared down a dark stairwell that looked like it could be the entrance to Hell.

I thought about finding another needy user for confirmation, but decided it wasn't necessary. I'd had this much of it figured right, so I was probably right about the rest of it too. I might as well go home.

That big pipe the boy had been talking about had run through Great Western Supply. Peter Johnson's death had closed it down, and whoever was running it hadn't replaced it. Not yet. They would, though, and soon. I didn't think they'd use Great Western again, but they probably would use some of the same people, and if Martha was up to her usual standards she'd have names for me very shortly.

It's surprising what you can learn from company records if you know how to go about it.

TWENTY-TWO

I CALLED MARTHA early Monday morning and asked her to meet me at the office before she went to Great Western. I wanted to tell her about my conversation with Jean Clausen and Larry Nichols. I hadn't had a chance to mention it when I talked to her Saturday afternoon.

I wanted her to watch for both names as she checked the files at Great Western. I didn't know what she could possibly find concerning Jean or Larry but I didn't want her overlooking any potentially important information because she wasn't aware of everything happening.

Also I had typed up a report for her to take to Barbara Johnson, and I had a couple of other specifics for her to see if she could spot.

I was beginning to have a generic picture of the man who had killed Peter Johnson but I couldn't put a name to him yet. I needed more details.

"I haven't found anything that could possibly relate to her," Martha said, referring to Jean. "What makes you think I might?"

"Actually, nothing. I'm just trying to cover all

the possibilities. I'm still fumbling around with the coincidence of you being kidnapped for Jean at the exact same time Peter Johnson was killed.''

''All right, I'll look. Great Western's modem capabilities are pretty good, much better than I realized at first. I tapped into the school administration's data base yesterday. I'll see if they have her name. I might find something about Larry Nichols there too. Maybe he's the one she thinks is giving information to the Janizarys.''

''I doubt it. I mean, I doubt if he could be the one. Not unless he's one heck of a good actor anyway. He certainly doesn't look the part. He looks like the original freckle-faced kid.''

Martha frowned. ''Is he kind of an innocent-looking guy, heavyset, with scruffy blond hair?''

''Yes. Do you know him?''

''No, I don't know him, but I've seen him with Howie. I've seen them together on duty, and I think I saw them over in the university district not too long ago having dinner.''

''Are you sure? When was it, and what time?''

''I don't know. I can't remember offhand. Maybe a couple of weeks ago? It was in the evening, but... Why? What are you trying to get at, Demary?''

''Knowing Howie, I just can't see him making

a friend of anyone like Larry. Larry thinks they're friends, you can tell by the way he talks, but I don't believe it.''

"Face it, you just don't like Howie," Martha said, sounding annoyed with me. She never has understood my feelings about him. But then I've never understood why she can't get along with Sam.

She left a few minutes after that. She didn't want to blow her cover at Great Western by being late.

I thought back over my conversation with Larry on Saturday. No matter whether I personally liked Howie or not, there was something peculiar about a friendship between those two, and the more I mulled it over the more peculiar it struck me.

I didn't like the picture I was playing with. I was still trying to fit it together when Cass came in a few minutes after nine.

"Hi there, sugar," he said as he opened the door. "Are you going to miss me when I'm gone?"

I grinned at him. "Nope. I'll be too busy chasing some other tall, dark, and handsome cowboy. Are you going back today?"

"Yep. I'm on my way out to the airport now, but I had to tell you good-bye in person," he said, making an exaggerated grab at me.

Laughing, I evaded his clutches, and barricaded myself behind my desk. We talked about the case for a few minutes and I asked him if he had heard anything new from his office in Texas, anything on the death of the two young men.

"No, not since I got up here. Why?"

"No reason. I just wondered. The two kids don't seem to tie into our case up here and yet I'm sure they are part of it. And speaking of kids, you said you worked campus security at the University in El Paso. Did you know Karl or Howie?"

"I don't think so. Or if I did I didn't know their names. I didn't pay much attention to the kids. They weren't my responsibility unless they destroyed school property. Were either one of them in any trouble down there?"

"I have no idea. I just remembered you worked the campus and wondered if you knew them."

Cass shook his head.

I went on to tell him about my meeting with Jean and Larry at the market, and about her suspicions. He agreed with me that she needed to confide in someone but there wasn't anything he could do about it. I wanted him to drop a hint to Sam. He refused, rightfully I guess, saying it wasn't his place to tell Sam something about one of his own officers. He also said that if I felt strongly about it I should talk to Sam myself.

Unfortunately I didn't feel I could do it either.

He left at quarter of ten, giving me a last casual kiss as he went out. His plane was due to take off at eleven and it was a good forty-five-minute drive out to the airport. We parted amiably, if not lovingly. I was glad to see him go. Brief as it was, the relationship had started off a lot more promising than it finished.

After he left I did some work on the computer, first for Harbor Insurance, then trying to evaluate scraps of information in the Johnson case that didn't seem to have any proper place. Afterward I started a master timetable for both murders, Peter Johnson's and Karl's. Sometimes it helps to see where each person was at any given time. I didn't know everyone's whereabouts at all times, of course, but I fitted what I did have together and filled in more blanks via some telephone calls.

I worked steadily until a few minutes before noon when I stopped to eat a container of peach Yoplait and listen to the twelve o'clock news on the office television set.

The first five minutes were devoted to some scurrilous political news that almost made me decide to vote Libertarian next time, and then the newscast was interrupted by a currently breaking story.

"We have just been informed that a Seattle policewoman has been killed during the holdup of a south Seattle liquor store," the newsman said. "We have no details as yet, but we understand the officer was a young black woman who has been on the force for several years. We will give you more details as we receive them."

The yogurt slipped out of my hand and splattered on the floor.

I knew the woman was Jean Clausen.

It took me twenty minutes to get through to Sam, twenty minutes that I spent either wishing I'd forced her to talk to me, or telling myself that I was being ridiculous. I had no real reason to think the dead officer was Jean.

But it was. Sam confirmed my fears when I was finally able to talk to him.

Our conversation was a total disaster. I cried. He yelled. I slammed the phone down in his ear. He called back. I cried some more. We were about as thoroughly unprofessional as we could get but eventually I calmed down some, and he quit yelling at me.

"Why the heck didn't you tell me what she was

doing?'' Sam asked in a tired voice when I told him of her suspicions about a rogue cop.

"Oh, don't be such a yutz,'' I said, hiccuping as I swallowed a last sob. I was mostly angry at myself for not making Jean talk to me—and for being a crybaby—but Sam was a handy whipping boy. "You know perfectly well I couldn't tell you. She would never have forgiven me.''

"Well, at least she might still be alive,'' he said cruelly.

That comment dried my tears. It made me so darn mad I wanted to scream, but it also focused my wits somehow. I'd known for several days that something was bugging Sam, but why a few un-related words put it together for me I don't know. It did, though. However, before I could say any-thing, he apologized.

"I'm sorry, Demary. That was uncalled for and I didn't mean it,'' he said. "She was killed in a gunfight with two coked-up white males in their early twenties. No Janizarys.''

"Are you sure?''

"I can't be positive, no; I don't have enough information yet, but I'm reasonably sure. She and her partner answered a robbery-in-progress call and when—''

He stopped in mid-sentence as someone in the

background yelled his name. The line went dead for a moment, then he came back. "Hang on, will you?" he said. "I'm going to put you on hold."

Several minutes went by. "I don't know what this means yet," he said when he returned. "But I've just been told Jean was shot in the back."

"In the back? How could she—"

"I said I don't know what it means yet," he interrupted. "She could have turned, started to move to a better position, any number of things. I just don't know yet. I've got to go."

"Wait. One other thing. When did it happen? What time?"

"A couple of minutes after eleven. I'll talk to you later."

I started to ask him when the robbery call had come in but he had already hung up.

I sat there for a long time, feeling bad for Jean, and wondering at the dedication that keeps our police forces going despite the danger they face every day, and the lack of appreciation they receive from the general public. To say nothing of the criticism and abuse heaped on them at every turn. That is not to say that every officer has an A-1 character. Which isn't surprising. Every organization has its bad apples. What is surprising, considering how many law officers are working the streets, is that so few of them are bad apples.

After a while I prodded myself into going back to work. Later I called the duty officer in my local precinct. Sergeant Owen Delany. I've known him for many years, longer than I've known Sam. He didn't like my questions but he answered them, and without asking any of his own.

TWENTY-THREE

AFTER I TALKED TO Sergeant Delaney I sat for another long time staring at the wall, putting the pieces together: times, places, people. I didn't like what I came up with but it all fit too well to be my imagination.

I was trying to make up my mind how best to handle the situation when Martha called. She had heard the twelve o'clock news also.

"You don't have to tell me. I heard it too," I told her. "And I talked to Sam."

"You know more about it than I do, then. I feel so bad. If we had only..."

"Yes. No. I mean yes, I wish we had made her talk to us but it wouldn't have made any difference in her death. She and her partner answered a holdup-in-progress call and she got shot. That's all there was to it. Shot in the line of duty." I stopped and swallowed, hard. If I wasn't careful I'd be crying again.

"That sounds like a load of codswallop," Martha said sharply.

"No, it's true. Or at least that's what Sam said.

Her death had no connection whatever to what it was she knew, or thought she knew, or to Peter Johnson's death either.''

''Well, I guess there's no sense in us beating ourselves bloody over it anyway,'' she said, sounding as if she was doing that very thing anyway. ''She knew what she was doing. She was a big girl.''

''She was doing a job. A job she chose.''

''Yes. I guess so. Still... Well, anyway, speaking of jobs. Listen to this and see if you think it means anything. I accessed...well, never mind how I did it, the point is I found out that several of the players in this game all went to the same grade school, at the same time. Deke Long, Howie, Karl Johnson, and Jean Clausen all attended Interlake. That old school right up the street from you.''

''School? Oh, yes. It's a mall building now full of trendy little shops. They were all in school there at the same time? Wow.''

''Yes. Actually, they weren't ever in the same grade at the same time but they did all attend school there at the same time for at least two years. Some of them were there for six years. And not only that, Lavander Starr—he's the one with the Janizaries—and Howie both went to Lincoln High School at the same time. They were in the same grade and had nine different classes together during the years they were there."

"You're kidding me. None of them ever mentioned knowing any of the others at any time."

"Actually they may not have known each other in the sense of being friends but at the least they should have known of each other when they were in the higher grades. Jean and Karl were only in Interlake for a couple of years when they were very young so it wouldn't be likely that they'd have any memory of each other, or the others, but, after talking to Helen, I think Karl did remember Deke Long. And that may have been why he particularly noticed Deke."

"That could be it all right. It bothered me, him specifically mentioning Deke by name, but if he remembered him from school, or if Deke had reminded him they went to school together, that would explain it."

"Now, here's the next thing. Both Howie and Karl were at the University of Texas at El Paso together, had a number of classes together, and they knew each other quite well. Well enough to spend weekends together. Karl lived in a fraternity house while Howie lived off-campus, but, according to the guy I just talked to at UTEP, Karl spent a lot of weekend time at Howie's apartment."

"They were actually friends?"

"In a way. The guy I just talked to was in Karl's fraternity. He said Karl wasn't much of a mixer but that Howie was a 'great one,' his words, for getting Karl to loosen up. And that he always invited Karl to the weekend parties he gave at his apartment. Invitations to which were highly prized from the sound of it. And also from the sound of it there was plenty of 'loosening up' done at those parties. With Mexico only a few miles away they had easy access to all kinds of drugs, and cheap booze."

"Well, well. The plot thickens. Howie did tell Sam he knew Karl, but I don't think he said anything about knowing him that well."

"It may get considerably thicker too."

"There's more? You have been a busy little bee."

"I got lucky and hit all the right keys. This fellow I talked to told me one of the other guys at the weekend parties was a campus cop. Which by itself doesn't mean much, but I also learned that Cass Feliciano was at UTEP at the same time."

"Yes, I did know that. I asked him about Karl and Howie but he said he didn't remember them."

"Do you believe him? I mean..." She hesitated.

"I mean, we have been looking for a second person. A second person involved in the murders."

"I thought of him," I admitted. "But it won't wash. He wasn't here when Johnson was shot and he came up here at Johnson's request."

"I wouldn't be too sure about Johnson calling him. That man is too smooth by half. I've been checking the phone log all morning and I can't find any record of Peter Johnson calling Valentine on Monday morning. The company uses so much telephone time with their modem ordering system, all Great Western's calls are automatically logged and timed, and a record kept on the company computer. But there is no record of him ever calling Valentine. Never."

That surprised me. I thought about it for a minute and then mentally shrugged. It wasn't that important. Johnson could have called Cass from home. As far as I could remember neither Cass nor Sheriff Tate had mentioned a specific time. However, finding the campus cop who attended the parties could be a help, and Cass might know who he was even if he didn't specifically remember either Karl or Howie.

"Cass is halfway back to Texas by now—his plane left at eleven—but I'll call him later on and see what he can remember about the guys he worked with.''

"All right. And here's one last item for you. It may not be important, but it is strange. Howie was registered as Howie Morgan and his school transcript is in that name, but all the time he was there he was known as Howie Bourassa.''

"Bourassa? That was his mother's name.''

"Uh-huh. And I got lucky with a bank in El Paso. The first one I tried had an account in the name of H. G. Bourassa.''

"Martha! You didn't access a bank computer?''

"Well, of all the bloody cheek! Of course I didn't.'' She laughed. "Mainly because I can't. Banking computers are too well protected. I simply called, gave them a fake ID, and asked to have a four-figure check verified.''

"They said it would be good? Four figures?''

"Right. They said the account would cover a four-figure check, and they didn't ask for the amount. Which means he has at least ten thousand in it, and probably a good deal more. So I might owe you an apology. Howie may not be as lily-pure as he acts.''

"That's for darn sure. That is a lot of money for a rookie cop to have in a bank in another state.''

I went on to tell her what I'd been working on when she called.

We talked for another fifteen minutes before we hung up.

After a while I went down to the Boys' Club to talk to the people there and to do a time check. When I came back there were still a lot of things I didn't know, but I was pretty sure I knew who had shot Peter Johnson.

Markie called at three. She'd hit the jackpot. One of the street girls had seen Karl Johnson having dinner in the Fractured Goose on Monday night. Karl had been with a police officer the girl knew by sight.

That tied it up. I didn't like it, but I'd been sure about his guilt for several hours now. I still didn't know what to do about it, though.

TWENTY-FOUR

STALLING, TRYING TO make up my mind what I wanted to do, I killed some time putting my conversation with Markie on the computer. I did it verbatim where I could. I keyboarded in:

"A kid I know recognized the guy in the picture right off," Markie had told me. "Kind of funny, really. She and a friend were having dinner when the two men came in and walked straight toward them. It scared the heck out of her because she recognized the cop first thing, even out of uniform, and she knew the boy she was with had been picked up before for stealing a car. The cop's name is Howie Morgan. She's not sure what precinct he works out of but she thinks..."

"That's all right. I know his precinct," I said. "Did she hear what the two men were talking about?"

"Not really, although they did take the booth right behind her and she could hear them. She said they kept their voices down

and she only heard a word now and then. She did hear your name.''

"My name? Are you sure? I mean, are you sure the girl was telling you the truth?"

"Yep, because I didn't mention you at all. I didn't tell her who wanted the information. She doesn't know you but she does know your name. Her folks live out by your office some-where. She says she catches the bus on the corner by your place and she's seen your name on the door. That was the reason she paid attention to what they were saying. She heard your name and kinda pricked up her ears. You know how you do when you hear somebody talking about someone you know. She doesn't know which man it was that was doing the talking 'cause she only knows the cop by sight, hasn't ever heard him say any-thing, but what she heard was one of them telling the other one that his father had an appointment with you.''

"What did the other one say then?"

"She didn't hear. Your name and the bit about the appointment was all she's really sure of. Does it help?''

"Yes, it does. She may have to end up tes-

*tifying in court, but don't tell her that. Did
you give her the whole fifty? It's worth it.''*

*''Yeah. I did. She'll just give it to that sorry
boyfriend of hers, though.''*

Markie had sighed. She isn't exactly a man-
hater, but there aren't many men she has a good
word for either.

I was finishing up the last of Markie's report
when Joey called. He was his usual incomprehen-
sible self.

"I got somethin' for you," he said. "Old Mrs.
Lewis who lives in 2C told me there was a cop up
there checking the fire door when she heard the
shots what killed the guy. She said—"

"Whoa, hold it a minute, Joey. Let me make
sure I know what you're talking about. You've
found somebody who heard the shots?"

"Everybody on the street heard the shots," Joey
said. "What I got is an eighty-five-year-old broad
who says there was a cop up there on the second
floor, in the alcove where the shots was fired from,
when the shots was fired. She don't know if he did
the shooting or not, but she knows he was there
when the shooting happened. When she first saw
him she thought he was going to check the fire
doors again; a cop comes by every month or so to
see if the crash-bar on the fire door there is the

way it's supposed to be. The building owner got
busted or somethin' once for having it wired shut.
So when she saw this guy go around the corner of
the hall that's what she figured he was doing.
Checking the fire door.''

''Did she recognize him? Can she describe
him?''

''Nope. She only saw his back. Good thing too,
'cause that way he didn't see her neither.''

''Yes,'' I said. ''But why didn't she report this
to anyone? Did she say?''

''She didn't say, but I know. It's 'cause she talks
funny. She don't like to talk to no one if she don't
have to. People make fun of her. She's okay in the
head though. I like her; she's a nice old gal.''

''Why did she tell you about it?''

''She likes me. I do little things for her.'' I could
almost see Joey smirk. ''Anyway, after I talked to
her I went around and talked to Bobby's little
brother again. I shoulda asked him about the shots
before, but anyhow, he heard them all right. Stands
to reason he would. Him and Bobby live in 2D,
just down the hall from the alcove. He still don't
know what time it was but he does know he saw
the cop in the courtyard before he heard the shots.
And the woman he saw in the courtyard was afterward.''

"You're a genius, Joey," I said, meaning it.

"I know," he said, modest to the last.

I told him I'd see to it he got full credit for helping me break the case and hung up quickly, before he could ask me if I knew who the officer was. It didn't dawn on me until later that the reason he didn't ask was because he had already figured out who it was for himself.

As I said, there were still a lot of things I didn't know, but I did know how Howie had killed Peter Johnson, and I could guess why.

Alone, or possibly in partnership with someone, Howie had set up a narcotics pipeline while he was still at the University in El Paso. Probably at the time Karl was working out the new truck routings Helen Wagoner told me about. Whether he got the idea from hearing Karl talk about the way Great Western trucks worked, or whether he cultivated Karl after he came up with the idea, was anybody's guess, but it didn't matter. No doubt he had maintained his friendship with Karl over the years in order to keep tabs on what was going on with the company, and on Monday evening his perseverance paid off when Karl told him Peter Johnson had an appointment with me the following day.

Howie already knew Peter Johnson had found the narcotics shipment but he could tell that Karl didn't know anything about it, so he figured he'd be perfectly safe again once he'd silenced Karl's father. He didn't know, couldn't know, that Peter Johnson had put it all on the computer.

The following morning he smashed Larry's watch—so Larry couldn't keep an exact time log—and left him in front of the Boys' Club with the phony story about establishing a snitch. Larry wasn't stupid, but he was naive and would believe anything his more sophisticated partner told him.

Then, after leaving Larry in the car, Howie went in the front door of the Boys' Club, out the back, and got in his own car. He'd parked it in the alley there before going to work. He drove up to Forty-sixth street, got into the Alhambra the same way I did, shot Peter Johnson, and went back.

The whole thing probably didn't take him thirty minutes, and wouldn't have taken him that long if Peter Johnson hadn't been early for his appointment. I'd done a trial run that afternoon in twenty-one minutes.

It must have given Howie quite a jolt, though, when he saw his target coming out of my door instead of going in.

Once I knew what I was looking for I'd had no trouble finding witnesses at the Boys' Club. Two boys and one of the coaches remembered Howie going through the gym, and one kid had even seen Howie get in his car and drive away. All of the boys had a pretty clear idea of the time. The coach knew almost to the minute. He was due on the floor to referee a game at one-thirty and had checked his watch just before he saw Howie walking across the gym, noting that he still had nine minutes.

None of them had any idea that the officer they saw had any connection with the murder committed blocks up the street.

I didn't know how or why Howie had killed Karl, or Dave Porter, or Deke Long either, but I was sure the evidence could be found. Arrogant as always, sure that he was too clever to be caught, he'd left a string of witnesses behind him at the Boys' Club and he had probably done the same thing other places. A little prodding would undoubtedly stir Larry's memory too, once he realized how he'd been used.

Actually, it was entirely possible that someone else, Lavander Starr for instance, had killed one or more of the others. Howie certainly wasn't running this whole operation by himself, and I'd thought all along that there was more than one killer.

At the moment, however, I wasn't worried about his possible partners. Actually I wasn't worried about him either.

Sam was the only one I cared about. I was pretty sure he had already guessed that Howie was the rogue cop; there was no other way I could account for his crazy behavior the last few days. But I didn't think he knew anything for sure, and I was positive he didn't have any idea that Howie had killed Peter Johnson. If Sam had even a suspicion of his guilt Howie would already be behind bars, son or no son.

I sat there for a while longer, rehearsing exactly what I was going to say, then called my local precinct again. It was ten minutes before six o'clock.

TWENTY-FIVE

SERGEANT DELANEY called Howie to the phone.

I think Howie knew what I was going to say
before I spoke, but he had to listen to me. The
phone was on the duty officer's desk where everyone could see and hear him. He couldn't hang up
on me. Which was why I'd called him at the precinct.

"I want to talk to you, Howie," I said. "Tonight. I know you and Larry take a break at nine-
thirty, so where do you want to meet me?"

"Uh, what about?" he asked.

"I think you know, and I think you know I'm
not meeting you for your benefit. I'm fond of Sam.
Well, where shall we meet?"

"Uh, wherever you say."

"No, Howie. Wherever you say, out loud, and
clear enough for everyone in the squad room to
hear you say the time and place. Owen knows who
you're talking to, and that way everyone will know
when and where we're meeting too, so I won't
have to worry about anything happening to me,
will I? I'm giving you a chance to explain, Howie,

and maybe a chance to cop a plea, but I'm not giving you a chance to get rid of me the way you did Johnson. So speak up; where do you want to meet?''

I thought for a second he wasn't going to answer. But he didn't really have any choice. I had a lock on him and he knew it. He didn't know where I was calling from, and if he didn't agree to talk to me I'd simply call Sam.

"All right," he said, his voice suddenly both charming and sexy. "I'll meet you on my break at that playground on Forty-third. Got to go now."

He hung up before I could say no. I wasn't too pleased with the idea of meeting him there, nor with the way he'd tried to make the meet sound. I would have preferred some more public place: a restaurant, a bar, or even a street corner. The grounds around the playfield were well lit, though, and it would still be fairly light at nine-thirty. It was too late now to make a change anyway. It would have to do.

I went ahead with my preparations. I added the conversation with Howie, and the time and place of our meeting, to the computer file on Peter Johnson's murder, printed out three copies of the whole thing, and got them ready to mail. I addressed one to Martha's home address, one—marked personal—to Sam's office, and one to Barbara Johnson.

As insurance goes, it wasn't the best, but combined with the call, it wasn't too bad either.

By the time I finished it was nearly eight o'clock. When I was ready to go I took my .32 out of the cupboard and put it in my purse, but changed my mind and put it back before I had even zipped my bag shut. I'm not for harsher gun control—we have very good laws on gun control now. Laws have never stopped a criminal from doing anything anyway, and certainly wouldn't stop him, or her, from acquiring a gun. No, my problem with guns is that I'm terrified of the stupid things. Rather ridiculous considering the business people think I'm in, but that's the way I felt about them.

I mailed the three packages on my way to a restaurant in the university district where I tried, without success, to eat some dinner. I wasn't particularly nervous about the meeting with Howie; I was fairly sure I'd covered myself adequately, but I couldn't get Sam out of my head. Twice I got up and started toward the telephone, wanting to warn him, to talk to him, to just hear his voice, and then sat back down again. I even thought about dumping the whole thing in Lieutenant Sheridan's lap—

he's head of Internal Affairs—but in the end I did as I'd planned.

The playfield on Forty-third and Wallingford covers two square blocks. The field house, public lavatories, and children's playground are on the east side along Wallingford Avenue. The west side is simply an open grassy area surrounded by wide beds of shrubs and trees. It was there, on the west side, that I parked under a streetlight. I had no intention of getting trapped among the playground equipment and buildings on the Wallingford side.

The sun was down but it was still quite light when I got out of the car, certainly light enough for Howie to see me, so I stayed where I was and waited for him to show himself.

He came out from under the trees on a cinder path at the southwest corner of the lawn and motioned for me to come to him, but I didn't move. Standing where I was, well in the open, I was clearly visible to anyone across the street who might be looking out their window, and I intended to stay that way.

"Aren't you afraid I'll drag you off into the bushes?" Howie asked sarcastically as he conceded and came toward me.

"No. Whatever else you may be, Howie, you aren't a fool." I kept my tone light, hoping to establish some kind of a reasonable conversational base between us.

"Thanks. For nothing. Now what the heck do you want anyway? I only came here because—"

"Hold it, Howie. Let's save time and get one thing straight right off," I interrupted, moving a few feet away from him. I didn't like him looming over me. "I know you shot Peter Johnson, and I know exactly how you did it. So let's just concentrate on what I got you over here for."

Howie gave me one of his supercilious smiles. "And what might that be?" he asked. He stepped off the path and leaned against a tree.

I stared at him for a moment, knowing now that I was wasting my time. But I had to try.

"There is no way you are going to get away with it. Howie. I've put the whole thing on paper. Names of witnesses, corroborating documentation—including your bank account in El Paso using your mother's name—and a ton of facts. It's all on paper, and all in the mail. Sam will get it tomorrow morning. So will two other people."

The mention of his El Paso bank account shook him; I could see it in his face.

"If you wait to be arrested they'll throw the book at you. They'll have to. If they gave you any kind of a break the papers would have a field day screaming favoritism. But if you go in on your own, give yourself up, offer to make restitution… Listen to me, Howie, I'm giving you a chance to make a deal, or to at least put yourself in a position…''

''You're giving me absolutely nothing,'' Howie snarled with a sudden burst of anger, thrusting his torso toward me. ''I should have killed you when you came busting into Karl's apartment.''

I stepped back a pace, a little thrill of fear racing up my spine. The look in Howie's eyes wasn't entirely sane.

He laughed softly. ''You didn't know I was there, did you? I was in the kitchen. I watched you through the crack in the doorjamb.''

''Wh-what were you doing there?'' I was furious at myself for letting my voice slip. I knew he'd pick up on it, and he did.

''Getting nervous, Demary?'' he taunted. ''And now you want me to fill in the blanks for you? All right. I'll tell you this much, anyway. I was looking for the last shipment, all right. You guessed that, I'm sure. But did you guess I found it?''

I didn't answer. He kept inching up on me, making me move back.

''Oh yes, I found it, Demary. Or I should say I found out what that jerk did with it. He flushed it down the toilet. Can you believe that? Over a million dollars' worth of pure coke down the drain. Not at Karl's, though. I went over the old man's apartment that same night, while his wife was over at Karl's with you. I found one of the empty sacks wadded up on the floor behind the toilet. Shooting was too good for him.''

I murmured wordlessly, trying not to sound as scared as I suddenly felt.

Howie grinned, his eyes glittering in the light from the pole behind me. ''Maybe this wasn't such a good idea after all, huh, Demary? Maybe you made a mistake giving me time to set something up. Did you think of that? No? Well, that's too bad, because I decided you weren't going to mess up my plans.''

His voice rose, almost shrill now, pushing at me. I took a quick look over my shoulder and stepped sideways. We had been slowly, steadily, moving back along the path and into the trees. Another minute or so and I'd be hidden from the view of anyone outside the park. I couldn't let that happen. I'd made a mistake, all right, but it had never occurred to me that Howie might strip his gears.

He laughed again. ''No, you aren't half as smart as you think you are, Demary,'' he said, making a sudden lunge at me.

I darted back, out of his reach. "Don't be stupid, Howie," I said, forcing my voice to a temperate level. "Giving me a hard time won't get you anywhere. I told you, I've already sent the whole story to three people."

"Did you send that black broad a copy? Thanks for telling me. I'll send Lavander after it. I should have let him at her to start with. Maybe I will in the end."

He made another little lunge at me, herding me into the shadows.

"Just a little further now, Demary," he said softly.

"You're crazy!" I yelled, losing my cool. "You can't possibly get away with killing me. Everyone knows…"

He laughed and came to a stop under a pole light, a few feet away from me. He was still out in the open in the middle of the path, and, if anyone was looking, simply standing there with his hands on his hips. "Don't worry, Demary," he said. "I'm well aware of what everyone knows. In fact, I made sure that everyone did know I was meeting you. And that's not the kind of thing I'd do if I was planning on killing you, now is it?

"Oh, no, I have no intention of killing you, Demary. I'm going to be standing right here where

Larry can see me when you get it. He's watching us from the alley across the street. That's where I told him to stay. He thinks he's my backup; he doesn't know he's my alibi. I'll be right here under the lights where he can see me while you'll be in the shadows and—''

''And I'll be right here behind her,'' Sam said in a tight, harsh voice.

I spun around, trying to place his position. For a second my mind went berserk with shock. Sam? It wasn't possible. Did I have it all wrong? Was he the rogue cop? The one tipping off the Janizarys? Did Jean know? Was that why she had refused to talk to him? No!

I sensed, rather than felt, Howie make a grab for me and threw myself backward, rolling to one side as I fell. As I scrambled to my feet again, ready to run, I saw Larry trotting across the street in our direction, and I saw Sam on my right, about twenty feet away from me. He was crouched in the shadow of a big laurel tree. Both he and Larry were between me and the lighted area around the buildings. Howie was on my left, closer to me, his face contorted with shock and rage, blocking my way back to the street and my car.

I placed them all in a flashing split second, and then, incredibly, Cass walked out from under the trees directly in front of me. He had a gun in his hand. A revolver that looked as big as a cannon.

The next several minutes happened all at once.

Sam drew his gun, shouted for Howie to surrender, and started running toward us.

Screaming senselessly, "Now, now, now!" Howie turned and raced off at an angle into the shrubbery, drawing his own weapon as he ran.

Cass yelled at me to get down and charged through the bushes after Howie.

Larry, calling Howie's name, vaulted over a flower planting and plunged into the shrubbery too.

All four men disappeared in the shadows under the trees.

The sky was nearly full dark now, the shadows inky. I couldn't actually see any of them any longer but I could hear them crashing through the bushes, yelling and calling out to one another. They seemed to be circling around toward the west side of the park.

I stayed where I was, backed up against a tree trunk, too stupefied to move.

Then, all shouting at once, they ran out onto the grass and came to a stumbling stop in kind of a half circle with Howie and Larry at the far side facing toward me, Sam, and Cass.

Sam was still pleading with Howie to give himself up, and for a frozen moment it looked as if he meant to do it, to give Sam his gun.

Howie stared at his father with a set expression. Then, without a flicker of change on his face, he screamed something, raised his gun, and fired twice. There was no way of telling which of us he was aiming at. It didn't really matter; both shots were lost in the trees. Cass fired a second ahead of him and the slug from his big revolver hit Howie square in the chest.

The force of the blow knocked him backward, spinning him around and down. He screamed again as he fell.

"You lousy, lying..." His words trailed to nothing. He was dead.

TWENTY-SIX

FOR A LONG TIME I just stood there, trying to keep the tears back. Howie's last defiant scream kept ringing in my ears. I wanted to cry for all of us. For Sam, for me for having been the one to hurt him so, and for Cass. I knew killing a fellow officer, the son of a friend, wasn't what he wanted to do.

A full complement of crime scene men appeared within minutes of Sam's call. He must have had them parked around the corner. Questions, answers, and explanations—futile as they were—flew in all directions.

Sam had been keeping an eye on Howie for days. He had not been sure of anything but he had put enough of the story together to suspect his son. And, as a senior officer, he'd been calling in old favors, getting some off-the-record reports from longtime friends. Friends such as Sergeant Delaney, who had telephoned Sam the minute he heard where Howie and I were meeting.

Larry had been watching from the alley because Howie had told him to.

Cass, bless his little buttons, had simply been worried about me enough to put off his flight for one more day so that he could keep his eye on me.

I went over my story what seemed like a dozen times for a dozen different officers, then, deciding there wasn't anything more I could do for anyone, I told Sam I was going home. They all knew where to find me if any one of them wanted me.

The house felt bleak and cold, with no welcome for me in any part of it. I wandered from room to room for a while, then made a pot of tea and carried it up to my bedroom where I lit a fire in the fireplace. A fireplace in my bedroom has always seemed like the height of luxury and comfort to me. Especially as Nora takes out the ashes and brings up fresh wood. Tonight it didn't seem to help at all.

I changed into a pair of silk pj's and a fleecy robe, and curled up on the love seat in front of the blaze, but nothing helped. I felt restless and dissatisfied, incomplete, as if there were still things I should be doing. I sat there for a long time, sipping tea and staring into the flames.

I didn't want to think about the case, or Sam, or anything, but bits and parts of the last few days kept drifting through my head. Like seaweed washing back and forth, caught in the tide.

After a while, out of a corner of my memory, I heard Peter Johnson's last words. Heard them the way they sounded at the time.

"Luck is a ventry fly!" he had yelled at me. It had taken me days to understand what he'd said; to separate the fear and anger from the meaning, to hear the words: "Look in the inventory file."

I thought about how Martha had misunderstood what she'd heard her kidnappers say.

It was a short step from there to Howie's words. They jumped out of my memory. A cry of rage. His yell had not been the defiance of a cornered criminal against a group of pursuers; it had been a scream of anguish at being betrayed by one man.

Not, "You lousy, lying…" Meaning plural. But, "You lousy, lying…" Singular.

And then it began to fall into place, piece after piece; sharp and clear as a laser beam. No doubts, no fuzzy edges.

I remembered the night Cass and I met Howie at the Half Moon Café. I had introduced Cass as Sheriff Feliciano from Presidio County, Texas. Thirty seconds later, as I walked away from them, I heard Howie call him Cass. They responded to my introduction as strangers; how had Howie known his first name? Later that same night Karl Johnson was killed, and a waitress saw a tall man in a hat standing near his apartment. Would she have remembered, or even noticed, the hat if it hadn't been unusual? Like a western hat maybe?

Martha said Karl and Howie were friends with a cop at UTEP. What could be more natural than for Karl to welcome that friend when he came unexpectedly to his door. He'd have no reason to be wary of him if that friend was a deputy sheriff.

And today. Had I signed Jean Clausen's death warrant when I told Cass about her suspicions?

He said he was going home. He hadn't been worried about me—that story had sounded thin even when I heard it—so why was he still here? How had he known I'd be at the playfield? And why had he been there?

Howie had been so sure he had a perfect setup. Him out in the open where Larry could see him, see that his hands were empty, and me in the shadows, a trapped pigeon, waiting to be shot and plucked. By whom? There was only one other person there. Cass Feliciano.

At that point my hands began to shake. I set my teacup down before I spilled the contents and told myself not to be silly. There was no way Howie could have persuaded Cass to kill me. Surely not?

It was nearly midnight when I went downstairs and turned on the computer. I knew I was right; it all fit together too well to be wrong, but I had to be sure.

I was standing there, looking at the screen, when I heard someone in the hall. It might be an exaggeration to say my heart stopped, but it sure gave one heck of a lurch. There are a lot of crazies around nowadays and I never have pretended to be brave.

I was almost relieved when Cass came through the doorway.

"Hi, sugar. You left your front door unlocked," he said, thumbing his wide-brimmed hat back on his head. "You should be more careful. Anybody could walk right on in."

That was a lie. All my doors lock automatically. They are never unlocked.

I tried to control my expression, but seeing him like that, just then, threw me off balance. And he read my face.

"You know, don't you?" he said. "I'm sorry, sugar. I really am."

"Know? Know what?" I asked, trying to stall. "Did something happen after I left? I just couldn't stay any longer. I..."

I made a vague gesture and took a couple of steps toward the phone at the end of the desk. I'd moved the darn thing down there so I'd have room to lay out some files. Now it was out of my reach. There was no way I could get out of the room without him catching me, and certainly no way I could overpower him, but I could, with luck, summon help if I could get my hand on the phone. Knocking it off the hook activated the alarm system, automatically calling the local precinct.

Cass came over and looked at the computer screen. By really bad luck, I had been looking at my notes on Deke Long's death and had just underlined the description of the elkhorn-handled knife found beside his body.

"Picked up on that, did you?" Cass said. "I was afraid someone would start wondering about that knife. There aren't too many of them around these parts. I didn't realize I'd dropped it until I was halfway to my motel. When I went back, the black-and-white was already there."

"You took a big chance, staying there like that," I said. "Or did you figure the big-city cops were all too dumb to catch you?"

Cass grinned. "None of them did, did they? And if that darn Johnson hadn't started doing a manual inventory we'd still be operating smooth as silk."

"Why did you go up there? To Albuquerque? If

you hadn't gone up there to check on those two boys' deaths he... Oh.'' I stopped as the truth suddenly dawned on me. Everything Cass told us about the deaths of the two boys in Texas had been on the report Sam received from Valentine County. That wasn't normal. There were always little details, unimportant little things, that an investigating officer saw or heard but didn't bother to write down. But everything, every single tiny thing Cass told us, had been in the report.

It was after I read the report that I got my funny feeling about Cass, my uneasy feeling. A feeling that had no relation to his sex appeal. My subconscious had been talking to me; why hadn't I listened?

"You didn't go up there at all, did you?" I said. "You weren't the investigating officer. And Peter Johnson never called you either, did he?"

"Right you are, sugar. Sheriff Tate was the one who went to Albuquerque. He didn't learn anything, but when Johnson was in town the following week and heard about him being there he started asking questions. One of our drivers told me. I didn't worry about him, though, until one of the guys here overheard about him checking the inventory Sunday night. That was a problem. We had just laid three cases of good Colombian coke in the warehouse Saturday morning. He found it, and as Howie said, he flushed it. I couldn't let that happen again.''

"You didn't kill Peter Johnson. You couldn't have. You had just gotten off the plane.''

"No, I didn't do that one. Howie shot him, all right. He didn't want Johnson spilling anything to you. He nearly lost it when he saw the old boy coming out your door, instead of going in. But he got the job done.''

"Why kill Deke?'' I asked, unobtrusively gaining another inch toward the phone. I wanted to ask him why he'd done it where he had but my throat was too dry. I couldn't get the words out. I knew I didn't have much more time. He would never be talking this freely if he didn't mean to kill me.

"He got wise to what we were doing and wanted in. Howie was afraid he'd talk even if we gave him a cut. Deke was that kind. And one of the boys saw him talking to a cop that morning in the warehouse. So Howie told him we'd give him a piece of the action. He set up a meet on the waterfront to discuss things. Between me and Deke. Deke was a tricky little weasel, though. He smelled something and got away from me there, and nearly got away again in the alley when he tipped over that barrel. Outsmarted himself, though; he was the one who slipped in the grease. He made Howie nervous. We had to get rid of him.''

''Just because he made Howie nervous?'' My voice rose to a squeak. I couldn't wait any longer. I was too scared, and the phone was only an arm's length away now.

Lunging forward, I hooked my fingers around the cord. As I hoped, he thought I was going for the window and simply jerked me to the other side of the room. The phone crashed to the floor.

Thirty-five seconds, that's all it had to lie there before the alarm was activated.

I struggled with him for a moment, counting one thousand one, one thousand two in my mind. At one thousand twenty I subsided with a realistic little whimper and let my eyes start filling. I always have looked good in tears.

I hoped they would distract him, hoped his unconscious reflex would be to comfort me. The wrestling match had changed our positions. I was now closer to the open doorway than he was.

And it worked. He let go of one of my arms and reached for his handkerchief.

Twisting frantically, I got my shoulder under his armpit, heaved, and broke for the door. If I could reach the hall I had a chance.

He grabbed at me, connected with a handful of my hair, and I was away free.

I raced for the front door, wrenched it open, and shot out onto the porch. Cass, a scant yard behind me, shook my wig free of his fingers and reached for the gun tucked in his belt holster.

I don't know what he thought he was going to do. He couldn't have gotten away; there were people all over the street. It didn't matter, though. One of the people was Sam Morgan, and his first shot smashed Cass's knee into a bloody shambles.

TWENTY-SEVEN

HOWIE'S FUNERAL WAS HELD the following Friday afternoon. It was a private service at the graveside. Sam and I and Angie's sister, Elise, were there. No one else. It was a depressingly beautiful day. It didn't seem fair that Sam should have to bury his only child on a day that was so bright and sunny.

We didn't linger after the minister's short sermon. I told Elise again how sorry I was but she just shook her head. "Better this way," she said. She nodded at Sam and left without another word.

Sam and I went to the Canoe House for an early dinner. I chose the place, partly to prove to myself that Cass hadn't spoiled it for me, but also because I knew it would be quiet there at that time of day.

We sat at a corner table where we could watch the sailboats tacking across Lake Washington. Beyond the lake, the setting sun was turning the snow-capped peaks of the Cascades into strawberry-colored wonders.

Sam ordered and after the cocktail waitress brought us our drinks we just sat for a while. I don't think either one of us really wanted to talk

but we needed to do so. Eventually, I asked him
if he'd found out how Howie got into the drug
scene to start with. I felt like I was poking a stick
into an open wound but the story was going to
have to be told again at Cass's trial, if nowhere
else, so the sooner he got used to talking about it
the better. The local newspapers had already had a
field day with the case. I'd had reporters camping
on my doorstep for days.

Sam didn't answer for so long I didn't think he
was going to answer at all. But finally he sighed
and said, "Probably in high school, after Angie
died."

"High school? Are you sure? I mean, he never
was a user; what makes you think he was into it
that young?"

"I'm not sure. It's just that now, looking back,
I can see a lot of things I didn't see then. Didn't
want to see, I guess."

I watched a speedboat, water skier in tow, come
streaking across the water. Thinking about Angie's
death, and about the way Howie had acted at the
time, I couldn't help wondering if her death had
really been an accident at all. Angie had been an
active member of a parents-against-drugs group. If
she had discovered that Howie was into the drug
scene, and confronted him....

I shivered.

"Are you cold?" Sam reached for the jacket I'd tossed on one of the extra chairs.

"No, I'm fine," I said quickly. One thing Sam didn't need was another load of grief. Angie's death was a long way in the past and now Howie was dead. Whatever had happened then was best left back there.

"Did you know we located the cocaine?" he asked.

"No. How could you? Howie said Peter Johnson got rid of it. Flushed it down the drain."

"He was wrong. And if you think about Johnson for a minute you'll realize he would never have done so. He was a sharp businessman; he knew we'd need it for evidence. He wanted it out of his warehouse, though, off his hands, but safe enough if anything happened to him. Which it was, and did. He didn't know who was responsible for the stuff being there, and he was probably afraid it might be Karl, so what he did was send it back. Then he came to you."

He paused long enough to frown at me. I had finally gotten around to telling him why Peter Johnson had come to see me and he still wasn't happy with me about it.

"He sent it back? Back where?"

"Uh-huh. He put a handwritten note inside and sent both cartons back to where they came from originally. Back to the manufacturers of the hot chocolate packets. We still haven't found the third case Cass mentioned."

"But what about the plastic bag Howie found in the Johnsons' bathroom?"

"It came out of Mrs. Johnson's travel bag. It was an empty sack she'd thrown into, or at, the wastebasket. She'd had cotton balls and foot powder in it."

I grinned. The idea of Howie mistaking foot powder for coke struck me funny. "So what happened to the boxes he sent back?"

"He took a marker pen and blanked out the triple X Feliciano's people used for identification, plus all the Great Western identification, marked the boxes to be returned, and put them with the outgoing merchandise. He didn't realize he had also covered some of the original shipping codes, though, and as a result they have been traveling around the country like a couple of lost souls for the past three weeks. They finally got back to Kansas City, where they started from, last Tuesday. Somebody opened them and from then on it was routine. The Kansas City PD called us late Tuesday evening."

"Whoever opened the boxes must have gotten a shock."

Sam nodded. "I'd guess they did at that."

"How did Howie meet Cass to start with? Do you know? Did Cass say?"

"They probably just gravitated together. Birds of a feather," Sam said, his tone bitter. "Howie was the one who set up the pipeline through Great Western, though. He knew Karl Johnson from grade school here, and once he figured out how to use the trucks he looked Karl up and started cultivating him."

I took a sip of my drink, thinking about Karl. He remained a question mark in my mind. "How about Karl? Do you think he was part of the deal, or not?"

"No. Howie and Feliciano used him. Howie kept tabs on the whole company through Karl. It's the thing that makes me feel the worst. Using a friend is a lousy thing to do; it's..." Sam shook his head, his expression tight and sour.

"Have you gotten anything out of Cass yet?" I asked. Talking about him still hurt a little. That was something I was going to have to get used to. Mainly it was my pride that was hurt, though. I didn't like the idea of Cass romancing me just to keep track of what I was doing and I had a feeling that was all Cass had really ever had in mind.

"Very little. He knows the drill. But Lavander Starr is talking. He's turning state's evidence and although he wasn't an original part of the pipe he knows all about it. He was another one Howie used. As far as that goes Lavander wasn't above using him—and did, to a certain extent—but still, it bothers me, bad, the way Howie treated his friends."

It bothered me worse the way Howie had treated his father but I didn't say so. I changed the subject a little.

"Why did the Janizarys kidnap Martha? Because they mistook her for Jean?"

"Yes. Howie found out what Jean was doing. He was afraid she was getting too close to the truth about him and his connection with the Janizarys so he told Lavander to take her out. Lavander says he was only supposed to frighten her, but that's bull. He or one of his gang had been following her for days but they never could get her alone. When Howie told him about her appointment with Harry Madison it was just sheer bad luck for Martha that Lavander sent two of his boys inside instead of going in himself. They didn't know either one of the women by sight so they took Martha, thinking she was Jean.''

''Cass killed the two guys in Valentine, didn't he?''

''That's what we think.''

''Karl?''

''Yes. We don't have any proof yet, and probably won't ever have any real proof, but knowing what we do now we have been able to pick up a few things. We have an identification that places him at the scene of the murder anyway.''

''The waitress?''

''No, a neighbor. She lives in the apartment building next door to Karl's. She saw Cass out her window that night but for some reason didn't think of him in connection with Karl's death until we did a door-to-door. She picked his picture out of six others without any hesitation, though.''

I watched a string of homeward-bound pleasure boats coming through the Montlake Cut. I'd held off asking my next question for days, but I had to know the answer.

''Jean? And Dave? Did I kill them both, telling him about them?'' I was sure it was my fault they were dead.

''No. We don't think he had anything to do with either of them. We know he had nothing to do with

Jean. One of the two dope-heads got her as she turned to move to another position. Her partner is positive. Dave is still a question mark.'' Sam took a deep breath. ''If he was killed, I think it was Howie. Feliciano had no reason for getting rid of him.''

''You suspected Cass all along, didn't you? Why? What tipped you?''

Sam shrugged. ''I don't know what it was at first. Maybe it was him being near the alley when we found Deke Long's body. I was never satisfied with his explanation, that he just happened to be wandering around down there looking at the King Dome. It was possible, but... Then, later, when I called Valentine, I found out that Sheriff Tate had gone to Canada for a month's vacation the same day Cass came up here. Cass was Deputy Sheriff in charge; he should have sent someone else up here, not come himself.''

''Cass told me he'd talked to Sheriff Tate. Twice.''

''He lied. We located Tate yesterday at a fancy fishermen's hideaway north of Alberta. He hadn't heard from Cass since he left Texas, had no idea he was in Seattle, and furthermore, had no idea why he should be in Seattle at all. Tate had not found any connection between the two boys and

Great Western beyond the fact that the witness had seen the Great Western truck on the highway a few minutes before he found the body. And he told Peter Johnson that when Johnson called him from Albuquerque. There was no reason for Johnson to have called Cass, and I don't believe he did.''

"No, I don't think he did either now," I agreed. I told him what Martha had found, or failed to find, on the Great Western phone log.

"I think it was Karl's death that first made me uneasy, though," Sam said. "Right here, in fact, when I told both of you that Karl was dead. The way I put it Karl could have died of a heart attack, but Cass immediately picked up on it as a slip and fall in the tub. That bothered me."

"Was that why you followed us home from here?"

"Partly. Partly I was just plain jealous too. Demary, will you marry me?"

"Did you ever ask him if... What?" My mouth fell open like an idiot. "What did you say?"

"I asked you to marry me."

"Oh. Oh. Well, uh, no."

"It certainly didn't take you long to decide."

"Yes, actually it did. I've been trying to make up my mind for days."

It was Sam's turn to do the idiot act. He gawked

at me. "What do you mean, you've been trying to make up your mind? I never asked you before."

"What's that got to do with it?" I asked. "And quit glaring at me. I knew you'd ask me eventually."

"Well, for Pete's sake. You might at least have let me think it was my idea."

I giggled, and in a minute we were both laughing. Sam's sense of humor, when he lets it show, is one of the nicest things about him.

"Sam," I said finally, "there isn't anyone else I would marry, but right now isn't a good time to ask. There wasn't anything romantic between Cass and me, but I did like him. It's going to take me a little bit to get over that. Ask me a month from now and maybe I'll have a different answer."

Sam looked at the dateline on his watch and signaled the waitress.

"Yes, sir," the young woman said, coming up to our table. "Are you ready to order?"

"No. I want to make a reservation for one month from today." He smiled across the table at me. "It's going to be a special occasion."

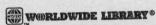
WGB392

Kathleen Anne Barrett

Milwaukee Summers Can Be DEADLY

A BETH HARTLEY MYSTERY

Ex-attorney turned legal researcher
Beth Hartley knows that history often
repeats itself—especially when it comes to
untimely death. The murder of a prominent
CPA sends a buzz through the historical city
of Milwaukee, and the desperate pleas of a
sixteen-year-old boy, the son of the dead man,
draw Beth into the case.

Beth's talent for finding the missing links leads
her to a solution as tragic as it is shocking, and
reveals why this Milwaukee summer could
turn out to be quite deadly for her.

"...you'll be at the edge of your seat..."
—*Rendezvous*

Available August 2001 at your favorite retail outlet.

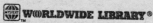

WORLDWIDE LIBRARY®

WKAB393

Camille Minichino

A GLORIA LAMERINO MYSTERY

When a janitor from a Massachusetts physics laboratory involved in lithium research is garroted on a dark street—hours after he agreed to accept a huge payoff for overhearing something he shouldn't have—Homicide turns to their prime consultant: feisty Gloria Lamerino, a former physicist from Berkeley.

With her natural ability to snoop and befriend, Gloria skillfully maneuvers her way through the upper and lower ranks of the facility and uncovers a hornet's nest of technical, political and environmental problems just dying to be covered up.

The Lithium Murder

"You'll love Gloria Lamerino and her friends."
—Janet Evanovich, author of *Hot Six*

*Available August 2001
at your favorite retail outlet.*

Elizabeth Gunn
FIVE CARD STUD

A JAKE HINES MYSTERY

It's a frigid winter in Minnesota, but detective Jake Hines has bigger problems than keeping warm. The body of a man, nearly naked and frozen solid, is discovered on a highway overpass.

As Hines probes the last days of the victim's life, a grim picture of betrayal, greed and fear emerges. But for Jake, solving a murder is a lot like playing cards—figure out who's bluffing and who's got the perfect hand, especially when one of the players is a killer.

"This series gets better and better. Gunn keeps her readers absorbed in the exciting case throughout..."
—*Booklist*

Available July 2001 at your favorite retail outlet.

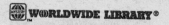
WORLDWIDE LIBRARY ®

WEG389

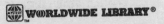